In 1983, aged eleven, I saw *Return of the Jedi* in the cinema with a friend. This was a time when short films were shown before the main feature, and also when the Cold War and the threat of nuclear Armageddon hung over us. The short before *Return of the Jedi* was an infomercial, showing what would happen in a nuclear strike; it said the warning given would be too short for many to get home to their families.

Hearing that, I didn't want to be in the cinema – I wanted to go home; I wanted to be with my mum and dad and brother just in case the bomb should drop. I didn't leave though, and the bomb didn't come that night, but the fear rumbled slowly along.

In the years following I read *WarGames* by David Bischoff, *When the Wind Blows* by Raymond Briggs, watched *Threads*, listened to 'Two Tribes' by Frankie Goes to Hollywood, '99 Red Balloons' by Nena.

Fear pushed me to try to understand.

I read what I could about Hiroshima, but this was before the Internet, and information wasn't so readily availab'~

The Cold War faded, I became a teenager, things changed, but the memory of that fear stayed with me.

Fast-forward quite a few years: more countries have nuclear weapons, more are developing them, and as the political landscape began to change and that threat began to loom again, I stumbled across an article about a Hiroshima survivor. It recommended a book – *Hiroshima* by John Hersey. I ordered it, devoured it, cried over it.

I had thought I understood what happened in Hiroshima, but it was nowhere near. I pushed the book into hands of others and turned to the Internet and to more books, documentaries, films . . . I wanted to know everything, I wanted to understand.

I looked back into history and I looked around at the current threat. What had we learned? Could it happen again? Had time muted the pain? Were we forgetting?

It was a moment in history that should still ripple through time, but was time fading it from our memories?

As a writer, I wanted to explore this. I didn't want to analyse who did what and why and all the should'ves and could'ves; what interested me was the people, the human stories, the survivors, the lost lives and loves, the futures missed, the regret, the sadness, the guilt felt by so many. The fear.

Researching it broke my heart.

I'm not Japanese. I didn't live through it. I don't know anyone who was there.

But I couldn't let the story go. And I kept thinking that if stories are only told by people who were there, then gradually everything will fade from time and memory. Some things are too important to let go; they should never be forgotten. We – everyone – have too much to lose.

Fear isn't exclusive to any decade, gender, country or culture.

Neither is guilt.

Or love.

The Last Paper Crane is about all those things.

Kerry Drewery

The Last Paper Crane

The Last Paper Crane

KERRY DREWERY

Illustrated by Natsko Seki

HOT
KEY
BOOKS

First published in Great Britain in 2020 by
HOT KEY BOOKS
80–81 Wimpole St, London W1G 9RE
www.hotkeybooks.com

Text copyright © Kerry Drewery, 2020
Illustrations copyright © Natsko Seki, 2020
Origami instructions by Nick Robinson www.origami.me.uk

A CIP catalogue record for this book is available from the British Library

ISBN: 978-1-4714-0847-2
also available as an ebook

1

Printed in Poland

Hot Key Books is an imprint of Bonnier Books UK
www.bonnierbooks.co.uk

Remembering my granddad, Walter Gage –
Lincoln Green, Tower Gardens, The County Hotel,
Madame Cholet with a penny in her pocket, Jack the musical clown,
Sitting on your lap,
A smile in a photograph.

We are
    all
    stories.

Me,
    my mother,
    Grandmother.
    My friends.

Even you,
    Grandfather Ichiro.

Especially
    you.

I used to think our stories,
    like our lives,
    are linear.
    But I was wrong.

They are circles
    among circles.
    Overlapping, linking
    together.

They ripple
    across life.
    But too often they fade
    from memory.

Your story, Grandfather,
    would have been forgotten.
    Lost.

But we saved it,
    you and I,
    to ripple
    across time
    forever.

PART ONE
Japan, 2018

My fingers glance over bent spines.

Blurred words.

Yellowing pages.

'Which one?' I ask.

'You choose, Mizuki,' Grandfather mutters.

I hear his grumpiness

I look up.

Rows of books across

rows of shelves.

Bowing from their weight

into smiles.

'There is magic in books,' I breathe.

'You told me that,' I whisper.

He scoffs from his bed behind me.

'Silliness for children.'

I sigh.

I miss what he was

before Grandmother died.

His lightness.

His smile.

His sense of wonder.

'But . . . stories –' I begin.

'Are only words,' he says, 'nothing more.'

I turn, shocked.

'Leave me alone.' His voice cracks.

'But –'

'Leave!' he shouts.

I grab a book from the shelf

and I slam

the door

behind me.

Our memories weigh

Heavy on our soul, like leaves

On a dying tree.

The book from Grandfather's room sits on the table.

My hand traces the embossed letters.

Inside, the characters drum their fingers.

Tap their feet.

Sigh with impatience.

'You can tell me your story soon,' I say to them.

'He won't read any more,

but I'll set you free.'

When I was younger

Grandfather would read to me.

Sitting on my bed, his voice filled the room.

His hand wafting in the air with the words.

His voice lilting with emotion.

When I grew too old

for bedtime stories

still we would share books,

still we would talk,

debate,

enthuse,

about stories.

Always stories.

But not any more.

When Grandmother died,

so did something in him.

I miss it, I realise.

I miss who he was.

Mother pours tea.

'What are you doing today?'

I swallow my yogurt.

'Library,' I reply. 'To study.'

Her fingers stretch around the cup.

'Can't you study here?'

Four words hiding a million.

The door creaks.

He shuffles in.

'It's a lovely sunrise,' he announces.

Smiling.

A good day for him?

Or only a morning?

Time will tell.

Mother frowns.

Worry scored into her face.

'Can you stay, Mizuki? I have to go to work.'

'Don't stay home on my account,' Grandfather says.

'I'm perfectly fine to be alone.'

We say nothing.

Either of us.

We know that minutes and hours alone

will eat those words of his.

I look at Mother.

Where's she gone,

my mother without wrinkles?

I nod.

Relief leaks from her in a sigh.

Her smile warms my heart.

Our guilt, it gnaws us,

Pesters, persecutes, till all

Is empty. Hollow.

As the front door bangs
    and the gate clicks,
    the clock ticks
    and Grandfather's face falls.

Shadows of the past
    pulling on his soul.
    What is in that head
    that affects him so?

What is suffocating
    the man
    who taught me to
    ride my bike?

Who teased Grandmother
    learning to jive,
    then tried to
    learn himself.

Who woke me

to show me

the stars

on a clear night.

Who played chess

with friends.

Made jam

every year.

Who smiled

and laughed

and lived

every day.

I miss

that man.

His fingers flutter

over the book on the table.

His palm brushes against the broken spine.

'There is no magic any more,' he says.

'I'm a bad person,' he says.

And walks away.

Out of the kitchen,

through the hall,

into his bedroom.

I follow.

The books on his shelves hold their breath.

What do they know?

What have they heard him

murmur in his sleep?

The smile of the shelf,

overloaded with weight,

turns to a grimace.

His back is to me.

'I did a terrible thing, Mizuki.

I can't hide it any longer.

'Your grandmother understood.'

    He lifts an arm,

    bangs his chest with his

    fist.

'She understood

    this

    pain.

    This

    guilt.

'She helped me

    bear it.

    Carry it.

'Now there is only me to

    remember.

    But I am old and soon . . .

    I will die.

    And then . . .'

He lifts his arm into the air.

    His fingers in a ball.

    And he releases them wide.

    A mime of an

    explosion.

'Even the memory

    of her

    will be gone.'

His melancholy,

    his sadness,

    his frustration,

    are palpable.

'I don't understand,' I say.

    'You mean Grandmother?

    I will remember her.

    Always.'

He shakes his head, and
bends to the ground.
Knees creaking,
he takes a box from under the bed.

'You don't know what I did,' he says.
'But I have to tell you.
Somebody younger has to
know.'

He lifts a book from the box.
Older than I have ever seen.
The cover is faded,
the binding is cracked.
Yet there are no pages.

He opens it.
I am mistaken.
One page is left.
He rips it out.

Folds it.

One way, then another.

And another.

Intricate.

Precise.

Motions he's repeated a thousand times or more.

'Listen,' he says.

'Then judge me.

Hate me or

love me,

forgive me or

condemn me.

But first . . .

listen.'

On the shelf
    he places
    a perfectly formed
    paper crane.

'And always
    remember.'

PART TWO

6 August 1945

GRANDFATHER'S STORY

I remember it was only a few days before my eighteenth birthday. I'm lying on the floor in my friend Hiro's house, reading, and I'm tired. Last night was a long one – air-raid sirens continually waking my mother and me. We have made that journey to the community air-raid shelter so many times we know the way in our sleep, but although enemy planes are frequent, not a single bomb has yet been dropped on our city, Hiroshima.

This morning the all-clear has sounded, my mother has left for work, and I plan to enjoy a rare day free from our mobilisation for the war effort.

Instead of making aeroplane parts, I have a book to read and a day to spend with my best friend.

I turn the page to Chapter Four as Hiro passes me a cup of oolong tea.

'That will take you a lifetime to read, Ichiro,' he jokes as he moves around the room, picking up toys his sister Keiko deserted before he walked her to kindergarten, a journey that on normal days we make together.

The book is *The Tale of Genji*.

I look down at the pages and remember when my father gave it to me, just before going to war . . .

. . . 'It was the world's first novel,' he told me, balancing the four volumes across both my hands.

'It is so long,' I said.

'Then your mind will be kept busy while I am away,' he replied. 'Promise me you'll read it all. It is a wonderful tale, full of love and guilt. Much to learn from.'

'I promise,' I said.

I remember that as I leafed through the pages, an unusual smile tipped his mouth and he leaned towards me, the smell of soap, shampoo and tobacco reminding me how long it had been since we were last that close.

'There is magic in books,' he whispered in my ear.

Yet as I turned to meet his eyes, he moved away.

'Tape the volumes together if you wish,' he said over his shoulder. 'What a pity it would be to lose the ending.'

So I did, and I carried them under my arm everywhere I went, reading whenever I could, listening for my father's whispers of magic . . .

Hiro strolls across the room and places a basket of washing on the floor; there are so many chores for a son with a father away at war. 'How many pages are there in that huge book of yours?' he asks.

I flick to the back and look at the page number. 'One thousand nine hundred and ninety-nine,' I reply.

He shakes his head in despair, for he is not much of a reader.

I turn a page. 'It isn't about reaching the end,' I say, 'it's the journey.'

Taking a sip of tea, I return to the words. The prose is as beautiful as the blue sky and yellow sunshine of the day outside, but my thoughts keep straying to my mother at work and my father at war, and to when I too will have opportunity to serve the Emperor and fight for my country.

From the corner of my eye, I see Hiro move towards the window.

'It's a B-29 bomber,' he says. 'But only one.'

My finger rests on page 348 of my book, marking the last word I will read from the 'before' time, and I listen to the distinct and familiar roar of the American plane.

Hiro turns to me. 'There's something . . .'

The rest of his sentence burns away on white.

A sheet of sun.

A flash of light.

Brighter than anything
I've ever seen before.

So complete it fills my vision
as if I've been struck blind.

Am I conscious? I think.

Dying? Or already dead?

Am I in heaven?

My eyes . . . they're burning . . .
my throat . . . my head . . .

My skin is prickling . . .
oh, now I am numb.

I am in the air.
I am weightless.

I am in an exploding firework.

Floating in air so hot
I cannot breathe.

'Gambare!' I hear. Be brave!

Did Hiro say that?
A rescuer?

Or was it me?

The flash is barely a second.
The 'after' is about to begin.

Waking brings little idea of whether I am alive or dead.

The light has gone.

The sun has gone.

All sound has gone.

Am I deaf?

Why is breathing so difficult? Why is the air burning my lungs?

My panicked thoughts buzz as if they were hornets caught in a jar.

I blink my eyes; grey swims in front of me.

Rubble? I think. *Bricks?*

I cough.

Lying on my back, I look up, but even the blue of the sky has gone, and the yellow of the sun too. It is as if the world itself has been blown away, leaving nothing but the emptiness of grey behind it.

Grey is everywhere. Deep, solid, consuming.

You must move, I tell myself. *You must get out and to safety. Find Hiro.*

I shout his name into the darkness, yet my voice is weak.

I shout again, but I breathe in dust, and I cough and splutter until my eyes run.

Come on, I think. *You must move. You must!*

My body is lead heavy. I wriggle my toes and my legs; I can feel them, I can move them, if only a little.

My arms are freer though, and I lift a hand to my hair, but wince. It is like needles being driven into my head.

I touch my face with my other hand but am sickened by pain. As I open and close my mouth, the skin on my cheeks pulls tight.

'Hiro!' I shout again, yet still there is no answer.

There is no sound at all.

I push rubble, long shards of wood and lumps of things I don't recognise off my chest and legs, and look down in fright as I realise that save for my underpants I am naked!

Who took my clothes? I think. *Where did they go?*

I stumble to my feet and, as shapes appear through the gloom, my mind struggles with what my eyes are seeing and all thoughts of my clothes and my modesty disappear.

The walls are on the floor, the roof is . . . I glance behind. I can't see where the roof is . . . the glass from the windows has gone . . .

The door? I think. *Where is the door? The table and chairs? Where are they? Where is everything? Where is Hiro?!*

My feet touch something flatter as I struggle to keep upright, and I catch a glimpse of colour.

My book.

I pull it out and grasp it to my chest as if it is life itself and can lead me through this nightmare I am in.

Swaying, and with arms outstretched, I stagger to the top of a pile of rubble and ruins and I look across what my city has become.

Everything is shrouded in thick dust and grey cloud, and as I look to the sky I expect to see the moon, although I have little idea if it is night or day. Out of the gloom, shapes appear, as if ghosts rising from their graves, yet these are not shapes of houses or people coming to see what has happened. They are shapes of piles of rubble, or of blackened tree trunks or telegraph poles, twisted metal sticking up like the broken ribs of a dying animal, or pieces of wood waiting for a flame to turn them to bonfires.

Desolation. Destruction. Ruin.

I cannot move for the shock of it.

The roads I walked along this morning are gone.

The carts that horses should be pulling aren't there.

The men on bicycles have disappeared.

The rows of wooden houses on Hiro's street . . .

The houses on my street . . .

The whole of my street . . .

And where are the people?

Where is Hiro's neighbour, Mr Hiyashi? His wife and children, where are they?

Mr Sato who sells us candy from his shop, where is he? Where?

I peer further into the city, yet dust and clouds obscure too much.

The shops of Shintenchi where my mother works? Do they still stand?

I look to the right. Towards the Shima Hospital where Hiro's mother works as a nurse –

Hiro . . .

Where is Hiro?

My hands shake. I am cold, yet hot too. My legs tremble.

Breathe, I tell myself. *Breathe.*

My body is covered in a million cuts, grazes and scratches. My back is sore, my face too, the tops of my arms . . . everything . . . hurts . . .

On the ground a few metres away, near where I found my book, is an uneven pattern of something different. Moving away the debris, I drag it out – Hiro's washing basket. Taking some loose trousers and a shirt, I pull them over my painful skin, and I take extra too, for, wherever Hiro is, perhaps his clothes are also gone.

Hiro, I think. *I must find Hiro.*

I shout his name, but my own voice in the silence shocks me, for it is so weak and sounds so strange.

'Hiro.' I try to say it louder, but the word is painful in my throat.

I step over broken glass, splintered wood, remnants of Hiro's home, and I drop to my knees and dig with my bare hands through the ruins.

'Hiro!' I try to shout again. 'Hiro! Hiro!'

I move a little, dig again and call again.

Nothing.

Now people are appearing from the rubble, as if they are the undead rising from their graves.

'*Tasukete!*' I shout. Help!

Heads turn my way but nobody moves towards me. They are lost in their own suffering and with thoughts of their own missing.

'Hiro!' I shout again.

Against the thud of pounding in my chest, I listen. I think I hear a whisper behind me, and on my hands and knees I clamber on, and I bend to peer through gaps and crevices and into dark holes.

'Where . . . ? Where are you?' I shout.

No voice comes back, but I see rubble moving and I pull at stones with both hands.

I create a bigger hole, and I dip my hands inside,
reaching, searching.

'Can you hear me?' I croak.

I feel the touch of human flesh, and fingers that
curl around mine with a strength that makes my
heart sing with hope.

Every piece of debris I pull away reveals more
of him, though it is not the friend who had turned
to look at me from the window. He has no clothes,

and save for one side of him and the lower part of his legs, his whole body is burnt.

Without warning, dizziness takes over me; I stumble, fall over, and vomit again and again until I'm shaking and sweat pours from me.

Fingers touch my back. 'Thank you.' The voice of my friend is thin and strained. 'Bomb?' he says.

'What bomb would do this?' I mumble.

'A *Molotoffano hanakago?*' he mumbles. A cluster

33

bomb. He turns awkwardly one way, then the other, looking, as I did, over the devastation around us.

'Not even a five-hundred-tonne bomb could do this,' I reply.

He takes a few tentative steps. 'This is where the garden was,' he mutters. 'This here, that I'm standing on, was the bomb shelter.'

He looks at me. 'Is it still day, Ichiro?' he asks, his voice quiet. 'The same day? I don't remember . . . I saw a plane . . . I was at the window, wasn't I? There was a parachute coming from it. I turned around to tell you, didn't I?'

I nod.

'Then . . . there was nothing. It was white, and then –' he shakes his head again – 'there was nothing.'

Without warning, just as it had come to me, he bends over and vomits, vomits until he is shaking, sweating and his teeth are chattering.

'I'm naked,' he says, when the sickness has passed. 'Where did my clothes go?'

'I don't know,' I whisper. 'I was naked too.

'Look at your skin,' I say. 'You were wearing your patterned shirt, your favourite one.'

He nods.

'Look, look at your side.'

His head bends and his hand lifts to his side, his fingers touching the patches of different-coloured skin. 'It's the pattern of my shirt,' he whispers. 'The pattern of my shirt is on my skin. But where did my shirt go?'

I shrug helplessly.

'What do we do?' Hiro asks. 'Where do we go?'

'I don't know,' I mutter. 'I don't know.'

We have no answers to anything.

I help him pull on the clothes I took from the basket, and together we scramble over the remnants of his home, thinking to head to a hospital, yet when we reach where we think the road should be, we both stop walking.

'My mother,' I whisper.

'And mine,' he replies. 'And my sister. Oh, what about my sister? What about Keiko? I should find her, I need to look after her. She's at kindergarten; she'll be frightened.' His eyes plead with me.

I try to think; I want to find my mother, take Hiro to the hospital, go to the hospital myself, but what about Keiko?

Her image appears unbidden in my mind; her dark hair shining in the sun as Hiro and I walk her to kindergarten, her wave as we say goodbye at the gate and turn towards our school or, lately, our military mobilisation, her giggle as Hiro teases her at home, her smile.

Five years old! I think. *She's only* five years old!

'We go to the kindergarten first,' I say. 'We find Keiko. Then we find my mother. Then yours.'

We step deeper and deeper into the swirling cloud; dust, dirt, smoke and fumes billowing on a growing wind and swallowing us into it.

I can barely breathe, hardly walk. My chest, my hands, my face, everything hurts beyond measure. At this precise moment, I can lift one foot, move it and place it in front of the other, but I have no idea how long or how far I will be able to continue.

From the grey of gloom, red fires spring towards us, blocking first one way then the next. We double back, cross remnants of roads, try another route, yet are beaten back time and again, and all this we do without speaking a word.

Words are inadequate for what we are going through.

I am weak, tired and thirsty.

Hiro's breathing is heavy. 'There are so many injured.' His voice creaks like that of an old man as we stumble past people lying at sides of roads.

'There is nothing we can do,' I say. 'Whatever we did would be too little. We must be selfish. Think only of our families.'

My mouth is so dry that my throat clenches together, yet there is not even a puddle of water on the ground I can lap from. 'Five people,' I say. 'You, me, our mothers and Keiko – we must think of them.'

'But my mother,' he says. 'The Shima Hospital . . . I don't think it's –'

'First,' I say, 'think only of Keiko.'

I hold her image in my mind as we struggle on, and I do not see or hear the people pleading for help, I see only Keiko's round face and bright eyes, hear only her laugh and her voice as she sings her favourite song while Hiro and I try to study.

Fires rage ahead of us, flames leap up into the sky and we're forced to stop at a road junction.

Hiro slumps to the side, sheltered from the heat

by a concrete wall. 'I don't know where we are,' he says. 'Everything looks the same.'

I sink to the ground next to him.

'Why are we alive and they are not?' he asks. His eyes stray over the bodies around us. 'Why am I burnt like this and you are not? What did this? What caused these fires?'

'Petrol?' I say. 'They could have dropped petrol on us and set fire to it.'

'Set fire to us with the *pika*?' he asks. The flash. 'But . . .'

Sickness crawls through my body and dizziness spins my head. There is no sense sitting here discussing what has done this. Fire is spreading and roaring towards us; if we are to survive, we must move on.

Standing up, and with my book still clenched in my left hand, I stretch out my right to support Hiro.

An explosion rocks the ground and my legs barely keep me upright as the remnants of a building close by collapse. A sudden blast of heat and smoke belts into us, and instinctively we duck down as low as we are able, coughing and spluttering as fumes choke the air.

Dust coats the inside of my mouth. I cannot swallow. I am so thirsty.

Yet I am caught by something else and I stare, over the bricks and lumps of concrete, to the white doorway that stands upright like a gravestone in the cemetery of a city, and as I realise what it is, I turn to Hiro and I watch his expression change.

From bewildered and barely conscious, his eyes come into focus, blinking and blinking.

He shakes his head. 'How did we get here?' he asks.

'I'm sorry,' I say.

'We were supposed to go to the kindergarten first.'

'I'm sorry, Hiro. The flames pushed us this way.'

'How can that doorway be all that's left of the hospital? Where are the walls? How can they just be gone?'

'I don't know, my friend,' I reply.

'She will have been in there,' he says. 'The all-clear was sounded.' His voice cracks as he talks. 'There would have been no reason for her to take shelter.' He stumbles over the wreckage. 'Where is she?'

I clamber towards him as he staggers forward; a step behind him as he falls to his knees, peers through gaps in fallen rubble, crawls further, moves some stones with his hands and shouts out her name.

He looks up to me. 'Where is she?' he asks.

I rest my hand on a clear patch of skin on his shoulder, then reluctantly I step away and leave him with his grief.

The collapse of the building has smothered some of the flames of the fires closest to us, yet across the city it rages on. We have to keep moving, but Hiro is swaying back and forth, clinging to his stomach, and his eyes struggle open then close again, time after time.

I stare over what is left of our city.

The castle has gone. All five of its storeys and its towers. Hondōri too, with its rows of lily-of-the-valley lanterns hanging over shops and tramlines.

And the university.

The theatre.

The fire station.

They are all gone.

Though some buildings, those taller or stronger or for some other reason I cannot fathom, do remain. The newspaper building, the beer hall, the bank, yet all, *all* with windows blown out or bulging in, walls missing or roofs collapsed. Blackened or scorched. Shells of what they were.

'Look,' I say to Hiro, 'isn't that the Industrial Promotion Hall over there? Its dome isn't green any more, but you can still see the shape of it.'

His head lifts and he stares across the ruins.

'If that is the Promotion Hall, and the Shima Hospital is here in front of us,' I say, 'then we need to go a little east. The kindergarten isn't far from the hospital.'

On we shuffle, as quickly as either of us is able, finding our way not by road or street signs, but by our relationship to the dome still standing and the wreckage of buildings around us.

Barefoot, we cannot walk on roads this close to the centre, for the tarmac is too hot, and progress is interminably slow as we pick our way over rubble, twisted metal and charred remains.

Flames leap from the ground and we flinch and raise painful arms to protect faces that are already damaged, yet onward we continue, turning back from fires and around from wrong turns, until we see the metal gates of the kindergarten in front of us, broken, bent and torn from their posts.

What had we expected?

I wanted it to be how my memory showed it.

A building in one piece.

Wooden doors painted dark blue, with inlaid glass catching the sun.

Children lined up in the courtyard with their uniforms and school bags.

Teachers in attendance, and someone holding a clipboard, marking off names of the children, who would all be there.

In my memory, every child is alive, and every one of them is smiling.

Our feet grind to a halt.

The building is all but gone. Only two corners of walls stick up, like white, bleached bones of a long-dead animal.

Where are the children?

Hiro limps forward faster than I thought him able, grunting with the effort and pain of every step.

'Keiko!' he shouts, his voice strained. 'Keiko!' he shouts again, staggering onward.

I stumble after him. 'The children aren't here,' I say. 'They must have been taken to safety.'

He lurches towards me, anger in his eyes and his arms outstretched, his shoulders and hands lifting. 'Where is that?' he demands. 'Where is safety?'

I shake my head.

'Look around you! Look at our city!' he cries. 'It's gone. Everything. Everything we ever cared about. Loved. Everyone. There is nothing left but... but... pain... and suffering. It's... it's hell. Hell on earth.' Spit flecks on his burnt lips as he shouts and shakes his head.

'There is no more Keiko,' he says, his voice quieter, his eyes glistening. 'She's dead. And so is my mother. And yours. We should accept it – it's just me and you now.'

I cling to the book in my hand, miraculously intact, and I remember my father leaving for war, the resignation hidden from his face but still in his eyes, the same resignation now in Hiro's eyes.

I remember my mother's smile as she headed to work this morning, and I look towards where the shops of Shintenchi should be, where she worked. There is nothing left, and I know with all my heart that she could not have survived.

I head over to a clearer patch of ground near a concrete wall, somewhere to rest awhile, but leaning on anything is too painful for my back, and I fear if I

sit down, I will never have the strength to lift myself to standing again.

The strangest thing is on the concrete under my feet, a dark shadow in the shape of a person with arms outstretched. Forgetting the pain in my back I spin around and see another further away, shadow arms raised to a shadow head. Again I turn, and there is another.

'What are they?' Hiro asks, his body held stiff as his gaze follows mine.

'They look like shadows of people,' I breathe.
'It's as if their souls are stuck to the ground.'

I stagger away, remembering Keiko; her smile
the last time we collected her while their mother was
at work, the pride in her voice as she announced us
as her big brother and his best friend, her laughter
as she turned to tell us we walked too slowly and
talked too much.

Oh, Keiko, I think.

My legs and my soul are too heavy to continue.

I collapse on a pile of stones.

Fires roar close, but I do not care.

I have little doubt my mother will have been killed, my father has been away at war so long he is not expected to return and Hiro's mother is unlikely to have survived.

And Keiko too?

I glance across to my friend; behind him flames leap across the ruins of the city that has homed us since birth and memories of our childhood billow into the sky on plumes of cloud and gas.

It is truly a scene of hell.

Fatigue washes over me suddenly, and I am so tired that I must lie down.

But my eyes refuse to close. The fog of my brain clears and I blink away the dust. Another pair of eyes, partly obscured among a pile of rubble, is staring back at me.

'Keiko?' I mutter, and I scrabble over the jagged ground.

The eyes become a face become a head become a person as I near.

I pull away lumps of stone and concrete with Hiro at my side helping too, and when we reach her legs it takes more strength than I thought either of us had to pull the concrete block off her.

Does she, the woman we pull free, see our frustration as we realise she is not who we are searching for?

My pain has not numbed my compassion, but it has taken my ability to hide disappointment.

So heavy is my sigh, it moves my whole body.

'Where are the children?' Hiro asks, but the woman shakes her head, and as tears run from her eyes, so water begins to fall from the sky.

'It must be from fire hoses,' I say to her. 'They've come to help us.'

But the drops are black and so big they hurt my injured skin, and at our feet the woman winces in yet more pain.

'More petrol?' Hiro asks. 'You think they're dropping more petrol to burn us?'

I rub my wet fingers together but there is no greasy feel to the water, and I lift my head to the sky, closing my eyes and opening my mouth to collect it on my dry, swollen tongue.

It runs over my skin and down my throat.

'It's rain,' I say. 'But like no rain I've ever seen before.'

The woman's mouth creaks open and her swollen tongue rests on her bottom lip, collecting raindrops that seem to be reviving her somewhat, and I do the same, cupping my hands in front of me and licking from them what water I can.

Why it is black, I do not care; it is wet and it is good.

Within moments we are all drenched, and as the chill begins to run through me, I see Hiro's hands tremble and the woman shake too.

'Take her over there,' I mutter against the hammer of the black rain, glancing to where the corner of a wall still stands with a fragment of a roof offering some shelter.

I don't know how she doesn't scream, for her left leg hangs from her as if it were a dead fish on a line, and as we lower her against the wall and slump down next to her, I wonder what the point was.

We walked past so many more like her and did not a thing.

We sit here now, the three of us, the rain around us, the air growing colder and us becoming weaker; little chance of help coming.

We are quiet.

The woman's rasping breath reminds me to breathe in and out, and when I hear Hiro cough, I am filled with relief that he is still alive.

The rain does nothing to wash away the shadows from the concrete, and as I drift in and out of unconsciousness or sleep, for I'm not sure which, I imagine their souls rising up and moving towards me with arms outstretched for help.

'The children,' the woman's voice mutters.

'To the park,' she persists. 'Those who survived.'

The words hang in the air like clouds on a windless day.

Slowly I open my eyes and lean towards her.

Hiro stares at her too.

'To the park?' I repeat. 'Those who survived?'

'Keiko Matsuya,' Hiro asks, a tremble to his voice. 'Did she go? Did she go to the park?'

He is shouting so loud she closes her eyes against him, yet she doesn't reply.

'Did . . . ?'

She lifts a hand, her face grimacing in pain.

'Please,' Hiro's voice is low now. 'She's my sister. Please . . .'

'Forgive me,' she whispers. 'I do not know.'

'We'll return for you,' I mutter as I struggle to my feet, words I mean yet cannot promise to fulfil, and as we clamber away from the ruins of the kindergarten, I hope a doctor will come to her aid. An ambulance or someone who can carry her to a hospital.

In my mind are clean wards with prepared beds, nurses bathing wounds and doctors administering drugs while family members hold warm spoons to thankful mouths.

Ambulances blare down clear roads that are easy to pass, collecting the injured on their waiting stretchers and hurrying them back to have breaks mended, cuts stitched and burns cooled.

In my fantasy, alongside the speeding ambulances, calm doctors and the happy ending I'm searching for, the characters from my father's book sit waiting for my reading to continue.

I clutch the book to my chest. A promise to someone most probably dead seems the heaviest promise of all.

Fires rage around us, yet we stumble on towards Asano Park, step by painful step, to find Keiko.

Can she still be alive?

We pass a tram, blue and red flames licking around its twisted frame.

Did Keiko walk this way?

Did her eyes rest on this burning beast?

Fire roars behind us now. I turn and see flames

leaping into the air, dancing on the wind and blowing towards us. The heat flashes on my skin and the fumes are intoxicating.

It chases us. Pushes us onward.

The wind picks up, fanning flames. Gusts lift sheets of roofing into the sky and fragments of burning wood sear through the smoke like a phoenix on its dying flight.

The collapsed wooden houses we run through crackle as embers light them like tinder.

I can't say the words to Hiro, but I can think them to myself. *I am frightened.*

We stumble into the park, alongside others now.

No flames touch these trees or bushes, but still I can smell and taste the fires, and feel their heat on my skin.

'It is safe,' I say to Hiro.

'For now,' he replies.

He doesn't look around to the fires threatening

at our backs; instead he looks to the injured lining the paths, glancing from one to the next to the next.

His wounds still bleed, his eyes sway in his head and his arms stick out from his sides like those of a rigid doll.

'Do your arms ache?' I ask.

'It . . . it is . . . too painful . . . to put them down.'

'You should sit and rest,' I say.

'Keiko . . . Keiko first.' His words are slurred.

His pain keeps me from focusing on my own. When my face hurts so much I think I will pass out, I look to my friend. When the skin on my back burns with the ferocity of the sun itself, I watch him walking, still conscious and still searching for his sister.

He is alive, I tell myself. *So must you be, and stay that way.*

His conviction and determination save me from sitting with the dying and becoming one of them.

'You think . . . Keiko . . . Keiko came . . . this way?' he asks. 'You think she's alive?'

'Of course she is,' I answer without pause.

I see that look in his eyes; he knows I am lying.

The possibility that she has not survived is a ripple in my thoughts, threatening to turn into a wave that I will not be able to control. For her to have survived the *pika*, the school falling, the flames chasing, would be . . . would be . . .

Yet here are Hiro and me.

I pull in a deep breath that hurts my chest so much I think I will vomit again, but as my step slows, so a flurry of cinders blows from the west as if to speed me along, showering my skin and burning me in pinpricks, and with it comes a blast of heat that takes the air from my lungs.

Hiro groans, his face contorting in pain.

'*Gambare*, my friend!' I tell him. Be brave!

I want him to sit while I find Keiko and bring her back to him, yet I fear he will fade away, or I will not find her.

We veer to the right and towards the riverbank.

'Please, help us!' I beg the injured as we walk past them, though my throat is too sore and dry for my voice to be loud. 'We're looking for my friend's sister – Keiko Matsuya. She would've come here with her kindergarten. They wear white smocks, blue hats . . .'

From face to silent face I look.

'Keiko Matsuya!' I shout. 'She's five years old!'

Still no one replies, and behind me Hiro loses yet more ground.

Again I shout, and again, yet still nothing.

I move deeper into the park, shouting, asking, stopping and waiting, for answers or for Hiro to catch up.

He slouches forward, his head dipping down and down before jerking back up, his eyes drifting in and out of focus, his body swaying left and right.

'Wait here,' I whisper to him. 'I'll look for her and come back to you.'

But he shakes his head. 'She is my responsibility,' he replies.

As I look away I notice an elderly woman at my feet, staring up at me with her mouth open. Her eyes blink as if she's trying to talk to me, and the finger on her right hand taps at her side.

I lower myself to my knees.

'Kindergarten,' she breathes.

I nod.

'No white smocks.' Her voice is barely a sound, and I lean in to hear. 'But children passed. Ragged clothes. Not good. Teacher said – stop at trees.' Her head dips to a clump of green some distance away, the darkness of people beneath them.

'Thank you.' I bow my head to her. 'May God be with you.'

As I stand I catch her last words – 'Today, God has lost.' – yet I give it little thought, for already I am hobbling on as fast as I am able, Hiro stumbling behind me.

'Keiko,' I shout with renewed vigour. 'Keiko Matsuya!'

At the edge of the trees I stare over ragged groups of children who stare back up at me as if they are baby birds waiting for food.

'Keiko?' I ask them all. 'Keiko Matsuya?'

At the sound of that name, a little girl looks up.

'My friend,' she whispers, and she lifts an arm

and points to a single tree tipping its branches towards the river.

Life returns to Hiro's body.

With some unknown strength, his head lifts, his eyes search and his feet rise and thump on the ground over and over as he runs across the undergrowth and to the tree where one girl sits.

I watch him drop to his knees in front of a body that seems so small, and I watch those tiny arms go around his neck and a tiny face tuck into his chest.

I look back to the girl – Keiko's friend – her head tips forward and her arms rest at her side.

Bowing my head in respect, silently I say my thanks, for Keiko is alive and we have found her.

The air grows hotter and thicker.

A sheen of sweat is forming on my arms as I hobble towards Hiro and Keiko, and as I reach them I see it on their skin too.

'Keiko,' I whisper with a smile, and the smile she

gives in return warms me like no other before.

'She's . . . not burnt at all,' Hiro says, his voice slow and croaking.

'Did something shelter you, Keiko?' I ask her. 'Were you behind a wall?'

She doesn't reply, and I can't tell if she nods her head or not.

Her smile slips and she says not a word to either of us, and as her eyes flicker from Hiro to me and back again I wonder what I must look like to her. Not the boy who helps walk her to school, brings her toys to life with a myriad of imaginary voices or reads stories while her brother makes her supper.

If my face and my back are as injured as they feel, then to her I must look like a sea creature or a monster of myth. Something awakened from a nightmare.

'There was a bomb,' I tell her. 'With a big flash and lots of heat. The heat did this.' I point to myself and to Hiro. 'It's still us,' I say with a smile.

Still not speaking, she points to her leg.

'Does it hurt?' I ask.

She nods.

As we've been talking, people have started moving, struggling back to staggering feet.

'Can you . . . stand?' Hiro asks.

With some help she gets to her feet, but her right leg hurts her so much that she can barely rest weight on it.

More and more people flood past us and towards the river.

The wind is turning violent.

The crackling of fires and roaring of flames tears through the air.

'We should move,' I say. 'Come on. Let's leave here. We need to find a hospital.'

More and more people appear. The air is hotter still. Orange reflects on our skin and speckles of burning embers fly to the ground we stand on. Some land on my book and I brush them away, but the cover is now pocked with burn marks, and the tape is growing sticky from the heat.

'We can't stay here,' I say. 'Hiro, we have to go. We have to move.'

I point to the tops of the trees.

'Look,' I say. 'It's coming this way!'

Yellow leaps into the dark clouds, orange and red too. Thick black smoke plumes into the already grey sky.

'The wind . . . ' Hiro says. 'Ichiro, it's . . . taking it . . . taking it everywhere.'

The smoke is thickening, the fumes overpowering, and the heat . . . the heat . . .

. . . my skin is contracting

. . . my eyes are stinging

. . . my lungs are burning . . .

I should've died by the bomb, I think. *Not like this, not by fire.*

I look from Hiro to Keiko.

But you've survived this far, I tell myself, *and so have they.*

But what do I do now? What do I do?

Think . . . think . . .

'Come on,' I say, and I bend down and scoop Keiko up in my arms. 'Hold this tight,' I tell her, thrusting my book into her hands. 'Hiro, come on, we'll go to the river. Cross to the other side. We'll be safe there. The fire cannot reach us there.'

Death has been chasing us all day, but hasn't caught us yet, so with the heat at my back and Keiko in my arms, I run now, because this is our only chance.

'Across the bridge,' I say.

Hiro limps along as I carry Keiko in my arms, my book clutched in her soft hands, her injured leg hanging limp and banging against me. 'Look across the river. There is no fire on that side. It won't be able to cross — the water will stop it.'

We stumble past others hoping for refuge from the flames. I brush embers from Keiko's hair, hold her head close to my chest and charge on and on, Hiro somehow keeping up next to me, a new energy now he has his sister.

Someone to live for, to breathe and to fight for.

We squeeze onto the crowded bridge, trying to

reach where flames cannot, somewhere I can find water for us to drink, food for us to eat. Where I can splint Keiko's leg so she can walk, where I can lay Hiro to the ground and wrap a blanket over him, sit with him while he rests, watching his chest rise and fall while he sleeps.

To the other side, I think. *Push on, keep going, clamber through.*

But we are not even halfway and we are forced to stop. We are surrounded by people, squeezed like rice packed in sushi or sardines in a tin; we cannot move. Not forward nor sideways.

I glance at Hiro.

'We'll have to stay here,' I say.

In a daze I stare over the bridge and down to the water below, watching a small rowing boat leave the bank, the oars cutting through the surface – one, glide, splash, two, glide, splash – while those lying inside neither move nor make a sound. I imagine the reflection off coins laid on closed lids as the boatman delivers them to somewhere they hope will offer peace.

The water is black and orange, the surface ripples and jostles.

On the bank, people sit or stand. A few wade in.

Be careful, I think. *The water rises quickly, and the current is strong.*

The wind blows hard against us, and as one the crowd of people tenses in pain and anticipation of fire as a flurry of burning leaves and twigs from trees, hot ash and cinders drops onto the rags of our clothes, on our exposed skin and gets caught in our hair.

I knock the embers from Keiko's face, but the pain stabs my hands like needles in my skin and the smell of scorching clothes from a too-hot iron, reminds me suddenly, agonisingly, of my mother.

The wind is stronger still. I look up to the sky – but the grey is all but taken over by flame leaping on the air. It is a beast roaring and mocking us, hanging over us, its victims and its prey, waiting to make its move, and we are powerless.

Again the wind blasts, and with horror I see that on the other side, trees are burning too.

With flames on both sides, we are trapped.

There is panic in Keiko's face as I look at her, desperation in Hiro's.

Think, think, think, I urge myself. *Come on. You owe them. Help them. Think.*

'Back!' I shout. 'Go back and down onto the riverbank.'

Going back is easier, for people seem keen to

take my place, yet I fear I am tricking them, for their chances of survival on this bridge are nil, I am sure.

You must think only of Keiko, I tell myself, *and Hiro and yourself.*

The crackle and roar of flames bear down on us.

The park is consumed by fire.

The heat glistens on Keiko's skin. What would she have done if we had not found her? I wonder, and as if she can hear my thoughts, she clings tighter to me.

'I can see the water, Hiro!' I shout. 'Come on. Quickly!'

He doesn't reply, and as I look over my shoulder at him, dread seeps through me.

'Stay with me, Hiro!'

I lead them down the grassy bank and toward the water's edge.

Keiko hangs on to me as we run, the book squashed between us, and I feel her struggling breath, the softness of her cheek, the brush of her hair on my chest, and in those seconds I realise that nothing, *nothing*, is more important right now than this little girl.

Above us, smoke plumes into the air, cinders and ashes carried on the wind, hissing as they hit the water.

I look up and see the people on the bridge, stuck now and helpless, for the wind is spreading the fire and the fire is consuming everything.

At the riverbank everyone is shuffling into the water. I squeeze between them, first one way, then the other, and relief spreads through me as I feel the cold of the water on my feet and my ankles.

'We're here!' I call back to Hiro. 'We're at the river. We'll be safe now.'

I keep moving forward. Keiko squirms, moves her grip, lifts her head up and looks behind me.

Her expression changes.

Her mouth drops and her eyes widen.

I see the flames reflected in her eyes and the orange flashing on her skin as it prickles with sweat.

'*Gambare*,' I whisper in her ear. 'I will look after you. The water will keep us safe. It will stop us from burning and we can wait until the fires die down.'

Yet I fear my words claiming safety are misguided; death has been chasing us, and now it seems death has us cornered, injured and helpless, in a river where I know the tide will be rising. I will not tell her that.

Hiro is at my side again, and we shove our way

through more and more people. Keiko tenses as the water hits her, and the cold of it is biting as it stretches and reaches up our legs, our stomachs and onto our chests.

My arms are growing heavy and my back is painful.

I look around at those we stand with. Behind me some are waist-deep, shivering, cupping water to their mouths to drink or clenching hands and closing eyes in prayer.

What will they ask of their god?

Some stand with water at their chests, others with it at their necks, one or two with it lapping at their chins.

So unbearable is the heat in the air that people splash water on their faces, on their shoulders and over their heads.

'Splash her,' I say to Hiro. 'Cup water in your hands.'

But his hands are too sore to use and he looks at me, full of despair. I nod to show I understand.

My arms are weak now, my footing loose, and I

feel as though I am a balancing act that could topple with one false move, but I must do something.

'Keiko, listen,' I whisper, turning to her. 'I'm going to try to lower you down. I want you to pour water on yourself, on your head and skin, like that man next to you is doing.'

She glances sideways to watch, but when she looks back at me she is shaking her head, her face a frown. She lifts her hand, my book, still dry, clenched in her fingers.

I stare at it.

The promise I made to my father the last time I saw him.

The last time I will ever see him.

Still intact.

It's only a book, I tell myself. *It doesn't mean anything. Take it from her and throw it away.*

But . . . but . . .

It is Keiko who solves my dilemma, for as I hold her, she tucks it under her arm, tight up against her armpit. The water may reach it, it may lap at it and wet its pages, but we will still have it. I can dry it, I could read it. I could still keep my promise.

Supporting her with both arms, I lower her towards the water, but with one hand around my wrist she clings to me as if she is a monkey, and her good leg wraps around me and I have to grit my teeth not to scream in pain.

Hiro is next to her, trying to help, but there is nothing he can do. Rather, she holds a hand out close to him, water cupped in it, and dabs it onto his face.

He closes his eyes with the tenderness she gives as she touches a cooling hand to him again and again, and as she lifts a scooped palm of water to his parched lips.

I watch the beauty that is sister helping brother, doing everything I can to stay upright while bodies on my left, right, front and back stumble and push into me, and though the current tries to drag her from my arms and pain rips through me, I do not let her go.

But the water is rising too, and those who had

the river to their chests now have it to their necks, and those with it to their necks are now kicking to stay afloat, but have little strength.

From behind I'm pushed deeper; I lift my chin as the water laps over my shoulders and I hoist Keiko up higher, the muscles in my arms burning from holding her.

Hiro bumps into me and stumbles, and as I reach out to grab him, Keiko slips from me and under the water.

Instantly I let go of Hiro, grab Keiko again, and the two of them splutter as they surface.

'I'm sorry,' I mutter. 'I'm sorry.'

Keiko looks at me, blinking and coughing, yet Hiro . . . Hiro sways on his feet with his eyes closing and opening and closing again.

'Hiro!' I shout. 'Look at me! Wake up!' His head drops forward and his face touches the surface of the water, yet instead of suddenly waking at its touch, he sinks into it.

'Hiro!' I shout again, and Keiko leans away from me and shakes at his burnt shoulder.

His eyes peel open and his head lifts to us, although I fear it is not us he sees.

'Stay with me, Hiro,' I say. 'Stay close.'

But behind us the fire roars and thunders its anger, forcing more and more people into the river, pushing us further and further, deeper and deeper.

My arms are turning numb.

In the distance, the rowing boat I saw earlier carries some away, although it is too slow and too small to save many, and as I watch it, I wonder where it takes its passengers, for it seems there is no safety to offer.

Next to me, Hiro coughs and splutters as the water laps into his mouth.

The push of bodies comes from behind again, and I stumble forward, my strength failing.

'Hiro,' I mumble.

His face stares back at me. He is so weak now, drifting away from me as people push, dipping under the water for seconds at a time, to resurface with barely a breath.

'Hold on to me,' I say to Keiko. 'Tight. With both hands.'

She looks to the book still sandwiched under her armpit, awkward and clumsy, stopping her from reaching around me.

'Let it go,' I say. 'It doesn't matter.'

She stares at me; a face of sorrow.

'Let it go,' I whisper.

Her tiny hand releases my promise to my father onto the water, and I watch it float and bob on the surface, but as she wraps her arms around my neck I forget it, for I must, and I reach a hand out to Hiro.

'I'll pull you close!' I shout.

I grip my hand around his arm and his mouth opens in pain, yet no scream comes out.

The tide is strong, pulling him from me; people are pushing behind and around me; Keiko is clinging to me.

My strength is fading.

Dragging Hiro towards me, my feet slip on the muddy riverbed and my stomach lurches as I'm plunged underwater.

Hands around me are pushing and grabbing, and bubbles of brown water and a tangle of arms and legs swirl all around me.

I cannot move.

Everything is dark.

Keiko! Where is Keiko? Up, I think, *up*, and I kick and kick, and I see lighter water, orange-tinged and red, and I kick up to it, higher and harder, and desperate relief fills me as my head breaks the surface and I gasp in air.

I grab Keiko again, hold her close as she too splutters against the water.

Hiro, I think, and I spin around to find him, but a sea of unfamiliar faces stares back.

'Hiro!' I shout. 'Where are you? Hiro! Hiro?'

Keiko taps on my chin then points, taps again and points again until I see him, some distance away now, obscured by so many others struggling just like him.

His chin tilts up to the sky, the water laps around it, his eyes drift closed, struggle open.

'Give me your hand!' I shout to him. 'Hiro, give me your hand!'

I try to reach him, but again I lose my footing.

In fear of going under again, of not coming back up, of dropping Kciko and losing her this time, I dare not move any further.

If I let go of her, she will drown.

'Come to me!' I shout to Hiro. 'A little closer and I can pull you in.'

His eyes open and for a second he looks right at me.

'Here!' I shout. 'Hiro, come here!'

His eyes move from mc to Keiko, and a sad smile appears on his face.

'No, Hiro,' I say, shaking my head. 'No, no. Come here! Swim here! I can grab you!' Again I try to move to where I can reach him, but the water is even deeper, the mud too slippery.

I glance to Keiko, and back to Hiro.

I dare not move.

'Hiro . . .'

The water splashes and drags at him. He shakes his head.

'No, Hiro, no!' I shout.

But he looks calm now, and I know his decision is made.

He bows his head to me and closes his eyes.

I close mine too and dip my head forward.

'I promise I will look after her,' I whisper. 'I promise I will not let her die.'

I open my eyes, and he is gone.

In that river I am a rock and around me the current flows.

Solid and immovable, I stand holding Keiko. Fires roar and blaze on either side of us and the air scorches the insides of our lungs and any part of us not covered by water. My mouth is dry, my thirst unquenchable. My arms are heavy, my legs are numb.

She clings to me.

Keiko.

But I will not let go.

I close my eyes, concentrate on Keiko's breathing, the comfort of knowing she is still alive.

A reason for me to keep fighting.

I drift.

My mother looms in front of me, my father in his uniform, Hiro as he turns from the window, white flashing behind him, as he looks at me across the water, his eyes closing, his head bowing.

As if sensing my sorrow, Keiko looks up at me, her eyes big and brown and full of confusion I have no way of easing.

'I will stay with you,' I say to her. 'I will not let go.'

The area is thinning of people standing, and by the orange light in the skies I can see across and down the river.

'Keiko,' I say, 'look!'

I nod my head in the direction of the riverbank a few hundred metres down. She twists around to see.

'The people there seem taller. They must be standing on something. There must be something in the river.'

She glances at me, then stares into the distance again.

'A spit of land?'

She starts to shiver; her teeth chatter.

I don't know what to do.

If we stay here, will the water subside? Will the flames abate? Or will we drown first?

If I try to move, will I fall? Drop Keiko?

Her tiny body trembles in my arms.

I take a deep breath, flicker my toes up and down, and my fingers too; I cannot feel them, but I think they are moving.

Keiko's skin is paling.

There is no choice. If we don't move from here, she is going to die.

I look at her face. So different to when I saw her only yesterday. Her hand in Hiro's as we walked her to kindergarten, her wave goodbye as we continued to the factory.

Only yesterday.

You will not fall, I tell myself, *and you will not drop her. You will walk through the river with her in your arms, and you will place her down on that piece of land in safety from these waters, and away from the flames.*

She wriggles and squirms as she wraps her arms around me, her body tight to my chest. I am numb from cold, yet I lift a heavy foot, move it forward and place it down.

I nod to myself, lift the other, move it, place it.

Yes, I think. *One step.*

Again I do it.

Two steps.

Three steps and four, and Keiko still clings on.

Another step and another and I am walking now, downstream, towards that spit of land sticking out into the water.

The heat is less intense, although horror swirls and bobs around me and I question again why I am spared and they are not.

Guilt lies heavy on my shoulders.

To save the life of the one in your arms, I tell myself.

Onward I move, the spit looming closer and the water level dropping down my body, yet Keiko grows heavier and heavier in my arms, her hands digging into my back. The water falls to my stomach, to my hips, down my legs and towards my feet and with staggering steps I collapse to my knees as we reach the land, scarcely a slither of ground to rest upon.

'Keiko,' I whisper, lowering her down. 'We made it . . .'

I am weak. There is barely the strength in me to swallow or to breathe. My eyes will hardly stay open, yet they catch on something in her hands, black and brick-shaped, swollen with water, pockmarked by cinders, bound with sagging tape.

'Father's book?'

She nods.

'How . . . ?'

She beckons me closer, and as I lean in, her delicate fingers run gently down my injured face.

My eyes sting with tears but I blink and blink them away, and I lie down next to her, holding her body next to mine to keep her warm.

'I will take care of you, Keiko,' I murmur as the world blurs away from me. 'I will not let you go . . . I will not . . .'

I wake to blue above me.

Stretched across a sky that I had last seen filled with black clouds, grey smoke and plumes of orange fire.

A blazing yellow sun too, bright even when I close my eyes.

My chest is tight as I breathe, and my head is heavy.

I close my eyes again and I do not want to open them. Images leap unbidden into my mind.

The *pika*.

The ruins.

Fire.

Water.

The dead and the dying.

Hiro.

Keiko.

Keiko!

I sit up, but I turn dizzy. Everything spins and I sway, my eyes watering and my head pounding.

'Keiko,' I try to shout, but my voice is barely a croak.

I try again but my throat feels as if it is ripping apart inside and I cough and cough, and without warning the ground is coming up to me and slams me in the head.

What is this? I think. *What is happening to me?*

Gentle pressure rests on my shoulder, then on

the back of my head. It touches my face and the delight of wetness is on my tongue and slipping down my throat.

It comes again, and a deep *shhhh* in my ear.

'Thank you,' I mouth, and as I bow my head in respect and gratitude and open my eyes, an elderly man looks down at me.

'The girl is here next to you,' he says. 'Through the cuts on his face and the bandage around his head, he smiles at me.

'When we brought you over on the boat, you wouldn't let her from your side. When we tried to put you in dry clothes, you refused until we had seen to her. And when we put a blanket over you, you removed it and placed it over her instead.'

'I don't remember . . .' I mumble.

He holds the water to my mouth again. 'The girl – she would not let go of that book.' He shakes his head. '*The Tale of Genji*,' he says. 'The world's first novel. It must be special to her, although too big, surely, for her to read.'

'It's mine,' I whisper.

'Ah,' he replies. 'Then she was saving it for you. Is she your sister?'

I shake my head. 'No. My friend's.'

At the thought of Hiro, I turn away. I do not wish this elderly man to see the tears welling in my eyes.

Yet at my side I see Keiko, and as I watch her tiny body rise and fall with every breath, relief swamps me.

'You saved her,' the man says.

I shake my head again. 'Not yet,' I reply.

Keiko edges towards me and I clutch her hand.

'Where were you when it happened?' I ask the man.

'In my house, eating breakfast with my wife. My injuries were caused by flying glass and brick. And from being thrown across the room.' He lifts a hand to his face and head. 'The *pika*,' he continues, 'the *don*' – the boom – 'after – I thought we had been hit by a meteor from space.'

'I didn't hear a *don*,' I say.

'I walked here from my home in the west to help.

The closer I came to the city, the more injuries I saw, and the more burns.'

'It wasn't a meteor,' I say. 'My friend saw the plane.'

'A bomb then.' He shrugs. 'But what bomb can do this?'

Again he offers me water, but I pass it to Keiko, her arms trembling as she takes it.

'I strapped her leg,' the man says. 'She should be able to walk, although not far, and only slowly.'

'Are you a doctor?' I ask.

'No, I'm a vet!' he says with a stretched smile. 'But bones are bones. Although you should go to the hospital, see what they can do for your face and your back. What they can do for her too.'

'I thought the hospitals were all destroyed,' I say.

He shakes his head. 'Not all. The Red Cross Hospital was swamped by flames yesterday. I saw it and went to help. For hours we fought to save it. It still stands, although not completely, but doctors and nurses are there.'

'There's nothing left of the Shima Hospital,' I say.

'There are make-do shelters at schools,' he says. 'But they may not have any drugs.'

'Thank you, sensei.' I bow my appreciation.

Pulling myself to my feet, I glance around, not at those lying on the ground with their injuries, but into the distance, where landmarks of the city should stand, to give me an idea as to which direction to head.

'There is nothing,' I say.

'Little,' the man replies. 'But ashes feed a fertile land.'

I struggle with his optimism, yet I appreciate the sentiment.

Keiko's deep brown eyes wince in pain as she stands with her left leg strapped to a length of wood. Yet as she limps and hobbles, she passes me the book and I marvel at her kindness and thoughtfulness.

There is magic in books, Father had said.

As I hold it close, Keiko pulls at the robe I find myself now wearing, and when I look down I realise she is showing me that the pocket is big enough to hold the book. I squeeze and force it in.

'You said the Red Cross Hospital still stands. We will try there. Thank you, sensei.'

Turning away, I concentrate only on the warmth of Keiko's hand in mine as we step from the riverbank and back into the carnage of our city.

Not a sound comes from Keiko as we stumble on.

On our right I see the blackened ruins of the Fukuya Department Store, still standing among such destruction, and I point it out to Keiko.

'It is made of concrete,' I explain to her, 'and it still stands, yet its windows are gone. As was the building you were in – concrete.' There are questions within my words that I cannot think to form.

Each time my fatigue and pain seem unbearable, I glance at Keiko, limping on and squeezing my hand, and I force my feet to keep walking and air to move in and out of my screaming lungs.

'Look, Keiko,' I say, glancing behind me. 'We've walked so far the bridge looks much smaller now.' I speak as much to alleviate the monotony of silence as anything else. She doesn't nod nor reply. Her face is a mask I cannot see beneath.

'Let's sing,' I say, desperate to fill her ears with sounds that are normal and belong to a time of happiness, the time of . . . before. 'Something . . . something . . . you used to sing at school . . . or at home. Something . . .'

My throat is sore from thirst again and my head pounds. 'What was that song? The one you used to sing all the time?'

I catch her wide eyes staring up at me, but cannot fathom what she is thinking. 'You know – the one that used to drive Hiro and me crazy. Was it about an umbrella?'

For the first time there is a change in her expression, but she says nothing.

We've taken no more than a few paces when she tumbles forward and I am not quick enough to catch her. Still she does not cry out.

Scooping her into my arms, I hold her to my chest and walk on. She is not heavy, but I am weak and fatigue washes over me, wave after wave, threatening to knock me from my feet and hold me to the ground.

'Not far now,' I tell her. 'We'll be there soon.'

Her eyes close.

'I remember the song,' I say. 'I can hear you singing it. It was "Rainy Day". You remember that one, Keiko?'

Her eyes stay closed.

'Course you do. You knew all the words. And the actions for the rain. How about you sing it for me now?'

She gives no answer.

'How about you sing as I walk? Bet you can remember it all.'

My feet are moving forward although I have little awareness of telling them to do so, and even less understanding of how they are managing it.

'Keiko? You going to sing?'

There is still no reply.

I don't look at her. I refuse to see what I fear.

'Keiko?'

I feel the tap of a finger on my arm and I smile with the relief it brings.

'Me?' I say. 'You want me to sing?' Her head moves in my arms in a nod.

In my imagination I see Hiro smile.

'*Rainy day . . . rainy day . . . I like it,*' I sing, struggling for air. '*My mother will . . . come here with . . . my umbrella; Pitch pitch . . . chap chap . . . run run . . . run.*'

On the last line her fingers tap the rhythm of the words on my arm, like raindrops, and I remember how she used to do this on Hiro's head and how much he would complain.

I sing the next verse, my breath shorter and more laboured.

'*Bag . . . on my shoulder . . . I follow . . . my mother; A bell is . . . is ringing somewhere . . .*'

I stop, and her fingers drum out the last line without my words, and despite everything, it brings a weak smile to my face.

As the song comes to mind so does a memory of her singing it over and over again, and of myself and Hiro being forced to listen as we slaved over homework, finding ourselves humming the tune as we figured out algebra or essays and cursing it for staying in our minds. Memory of a simpler time; before mobilisation and military planes in the sky.

I struggle on through the next two verses, each time her fingers tapping out the last line as if they were the rain, yet as we reach the last verse my memory is blank.

'I can't remember it, Keiko.'

I look down. Her eyes are closed.

'Can you?'

She shakes her head.

'Never mind,' I say. 'We haven't far to go now.'

But as I look across the ruins, the hospital still seems a long, long way to go.

I become unaware of the pleadings of those we pass, focusing only on the dark building of our sanctuary, the walls around it, the tower rising up in the middle, but countless times too much rubble, charred wood or remnants of houses block our path and the only way forward is to go sideways.

The hospital moves.

Doubt floods me.

We're not going to make it, I think. *I cannot carry Keiko all that way.*

My feet slow.

Yes, I tell myself. *Yes, you can.*

I force myself onward, but it is only a few more paces before again I stumble and we both fall in a heap on the ground.

I lean Keiko gently against the burnt-out carcass of a tram, brush the dirt from her face and the dust from her hair.

Should we rest? I think. *Before we carry on?*

I look at Keiko, then across the ruins of our city to the hospital in the distance. Still so far.

I know in my heart that I cannot carry her such a distance.

If I can get there at least, I think, *there will be doctors there. Stretchers. And people stronger than me. Who could come back and help.*

But to go means I would have to . . . leave Keiko on her own . . .

My mind reels at the idea.

Think, think, think, I tell myself, but however hard I try, I cannot see another way.

Dragging in a painful breath, I turn to her.

'Keiko,' I say, 'the hospital's still quite far . . . You can't walk any further . . . That's fine . . . but . . . I don't have the strength . . . to carry you all that way.' I pause, take another breath. 'If you wait here, I can . . . get help . . . bring a doctor or a . . . nurse . . . with a stretcher to carry you.'

Her brown eyes, full of trust, stare into mine and I have to look away.

'I promise . . . I'll return,' I say. 'Promise.'

A few other people are sitting close by; a woman with a young boy, two people with few marks on their faces but badly burnt hands, a man dressed only in rags.

'Be brave,' I say, touching her hand. 'I'll be back as . . . soon as . . . I can. I promise.'

I drag myself to standing, but I feel sick with what I'm doing.

Is this my only choice?

I take one last look over my shoulder, and she seems so sad and vulnerable that I stop.

I flick at the tattered pages of the book in my pocket.

Turning and taking a few paces back, I stumble down next to her again and open the book.

'My father gave me this . . . the day he went to war,' I tell her. 'I promised . . . I'd read it . . . before he . . . came home. But . . .'

I peel the wet pages apart and carefully tear out the first page, as her eyes widen in horror. Through my cracked, dry skin I try to smile at her. 'It's OK – I've read this page. 'My father, he . . . read all the time and he . . . told me there is . . . magic in books.'

I close the book, place the loose page on top and, with shaking hands, start to fold.

'I'm going to go . . . get help, but . . . I'm going to leave a bit of magic here.' I smile at her again. 'To look after . . . you.'

Despite how tired she is, and how ill she looks, she leans forward and watches my clumsy fingers struggling with folds and creases in the damp paper.

When I'm finished, I place the paper bird on her lap. 'A crane,' I say.

Her face lightens and she lifts a finger, beckoning me closer.

'What?' I ask.

Closer and closer she beckons me, until my ear is at her lips, and I hear the quietest of whispers, that is barely breath upon my skin.

'*I am all right, don't worry,*' she sings. '*Mother will take me in her big umbrella . . . pitch pitch . . . chap chap . . . run run run.*' As she says the last line of the song, her fingers tap on my hand like rain.

'The final verse,' I whisper as I lean back to see her face. 'You remembered . . . the final verse!'

A hint of a smile flickers at her mouth as finally she speaks. 'Yes, Ichiro Ando.'

With my book again in my pocket, I stand, and I'm nodding now, although not only to comfort her. 'I will be back as soon as I can,' I say. 'Don't worry.'

I look at her, and with a lump in my throat I whisper the words 'I promise' one last time and I mean them with all my heart.

Don't look back, I tell myself. *Don't look back*.

The sun beats down.

I'm thirsty.

Tired.

My mind swims; shows me Keiko watching me disappear into the distance.

The pain of leaving her tears at me more than any bomb ever could.

I close my eyes for a few steps, open them again to make sure I'm still moving in the right direction.

A woman with my mother's face shuffles towards me and my heart lifts, only to drop like lead as it blurs into someone else.

Closing my eyes again, I stumble on.

Hiro is next to me.

'You left her,' he says.

'I had to,' I reply. 'We wouldn't have made it. This is the only way.'

'You promised,' he says, before he disappears.

I open my eyes. The hospital is closer. I can make out the broken windows, the burn marks from the fire.

I stare at it and it blurs.

'You're nearly there.' Hiro's voice, loud in my head.

'I'm tired,' I reply. 'More tired than I've ever been in my life. I want to sit . . . sleep.'

'Soon,' he says.

A little further and beside me is my father; the smell of soap, shampoo, boot polish and tobacco.

'You think a book is more important than a life?' he asks.

'I made a promise to you,' I reply.

'And you made a promise to your best friend! To look after his little sister!'

I shake my head. 'I'm taking care of my promises,' I insist, but there is doubt in my heart.

Onward and onward, until finally I'm clambering over the wreckage and debris surrounding the gates.

My feet are lighter because there is the end.

There.

There are the doors and I'm touching them.

I'm pushing them open and I'm going inside.

Inside.

People are everywhere; standing, sitting, lying, crouching.

On concrete. Straw. Tatami mats. Packed in.

'Where's a doctor?' I shout. 'Please . . . my friend . . . needs help. She's dying.'

'Aren't we all?' a voice croaks at my feet.

I stumble along the corridor.

'Doctor? Please . . . or nurse . . . please . . . someone. She's only five . . . five years old.'

I pull open a door and find myself in a ward. Not a single piece of floor is uncovered, nor a single bed unoccupied. Only one patient – a woman –

turns to me, her lips cracked and eyes pleading.

'Water?' she says.

Water, I think. *Yes, that would be good.*

Out of the ward I stagger down another corridor.

'Doctor!' I shout. 'Please . . . I need . . . need a doctor for my friend, a little girl. Please!'

Up a staircase I climb, clambering over yet more people. Pushing open a door, I find a storage room, people in there too.

Another door to a toilet, and again more waiting to be treated.

I see Keiko in my mind. Worried and hurting. Scared.

How long have I been gone?

I push open another door, look into another full ward, close it again and move on. Another door shows an office with sheets on the floor as makeshift beds, and there, among the injured, crouches a solitary man with caring eyes and a dirty white coat.

'Doctor?' I breathe.

He turns to me, his face full of tiny cuts. 'Yes,' he replies.

I bow as deep as I am able. 'Please,' I mutter, but as I try to straighten up, the ward sways and my legs buckle underneath me.

Yet he is at my side, his arms holding and guiding me to a space on the floor, and although it is barely large enough to sit on, I am thankful beyond belief.

'Please,' I say again. 'My friend's sister's hurt . . . her leg's injured . . . maybe broken . . . I couldn't carry her any . . . further.'

There is not enough air in me to speak so much. I breathe in, out, in again. 'I had to leave her,' I say. 'Next to a burnt-out tram . . . on the Ujina line.' I try to raise a hand to point, but I have no strength.

'Shhhh,' he says, taking my hand and easing it down. 'Steady.'

He offers water to my mouth and it is like heaven. Relief flows through me and my skin prickles with sheer emotion.

'Thank you,' I say. 'Thank you. Thank you.' But no matter how many times I say the words, they are inadequate.

Again he lifts the cup to my lips.

'Take your time,' he tells me, but I shake my head because there is no time.

'She's not burnt,' I say as I look at him, his thin face lined with wisdom, his short hair streaked with grey, the understanding and the pain in his eyes. 'She was in the school. There was concrete all around her.'

He nods.

'Her leg's been splinted. She walked as far as she could, and I carried her, but . . .'

He puts the water to my mouth again and I sip it.

'I told her I would come for help . . . go back for her . . .'

His face doesn't move.

'Can you help me? Please.'

He sucks in a deep breath and his lips stretch thin.

'I promised her I'd go back for her . . . I'm not sure how far it is . . . past the Shirakami-mae station . . . maybe a mile from here . . . maybe less, I'm not sure . . .'

I hear the air seep from his lungs as a sigh.

'In this hospital today are six doctors,' he says, his voice calm and quiet. 'Usually there are thirty. Of those six, I am the least injured.'

'A nurse then,' I plead.

His face tenses. 'We have ten of our normal two hundred.'

'But –'

'Where the others are, I could not tell you. I fear they are dead because I know each would be here if they were able. We are more than full with patients, I'm sure you've seen, but more appear every minute. Did you see all the people outside?'

I nod.

'Yes,' he says. 'A frightful sight.' His hands lift then clasp together again. 'And some of the people in the corridors or on the wards have already died too, but they stay there because we haven't had the time to move them and, quite frankly, I'm not sure where we would put them.'

'I could help you,' I say. 'I could –'

He lifts a hand to stop me. 'Young man, you are very ill, and although we all are ill, or injured, you cannot –'

'Please, I need to get help to Keiko. I need you, or . . . or . . . or someone to come back with me . . . to . . . Please . . . she's on the Ujina line.' I try to pull myself up, but my knees buckle and I'm on the floor again.

'Young man.' There's a strain to his voice. 'Please try to understand my predicament. In the time it would take me to walk to your friend and bring her back, I could have treated more than twenty people in here. Thirty maybe, depending on what I could do for them.'

'But I –'

'No, you cannot, and although it distresses me to say this, I cannot leave the hospital to treat your friend. How could I walk past thousands, to save one? As her friend, you can do that. As a doctor, I cannot.

'With all my heart I am sorry,' he continues. 'You

and your friend deserve more, but so does everyone else. You can stay, and I will treat you and look after you as best as I am able, but –'

I shake my head. 'I need to get back to her. I cannot desert her.'

I struggle to my feet.

He supports me as I regain my balance, and holds the cup to my mouth as I drink the last of the water.

'I wish it could be different,' he says, and as he opens the door for me, he reaches into his pocket and pulls out a tomato, red and ripe and shiny.

My eyes widen at the sight of it.

'Take this for your friend,' he says.

I slip it into my pocket and bow my thanks.

I stumble along the corridor.

Why did I leave her? I think.

Past and over people sprawled across the dirty floor.

I've gained nothing.

Down stairs that tilt and turn before my eyes

and I step on softness that must be arms or legs, yet nobody screams.

She would be here with me now.

Bright light shines from the end of the corridor and I lumber towards it, bouncing off walls, hands pushing me away.

How could I have left her?

Out of the doors and into blazing sunlight, but everything blurs; I can't see the tramlines. Can't see anything. Recognise nothing.

I am coming, Keiko.

Panic swims through me. My head pounds. My legs buckle. I fall to the ground. Something squashes into me. I look down – red of the split tomato. Sadness fills me – a ruined act of kindness. My stomach pulls. I vomit and vomit.

I will save you.

I stand again, but the world shakes . . . turns black . . . slams against my knees.

Keiko.

Crawl forward . . . try to stand . . . legs gone . . . . . . arms weak . . .

. . . can't keep head up . . .

. . . can't move . . .

Kurushī – I'm done.

. . . there's nothing . . . save for the one thing I failed to do . . .

'Keiko,' I breathe.

I open my eyes to a darkened room lit by the flickering light of a candle.

Shadows leap across the walls around me like ghosts of the lost, searching for an explanation or reason, and I imagine their rasping voices pleading for news of friends or neighbours, husbands or wives, sons or daughters.

I wish I had answers for them. I wish I could heal their pain. But I cannot.

I slip off the bed, and tiptoe across to a large window, the wind blowing in through the missing glass.

My head is clear and I stare into the blackness

below, where my city and my home once were, now filled with horror and pain.

'Why should I live when you do not?' I say.

Patches of orange and yellow flame dot against the black, and grey smoke drifts into the night sky.

I lift myself onto the ledge of the window, swing my legs around and sit there.

My body is heavy with the guilt of surviving.

The wind picks up, and with it comes a thousand pages of a book, blowing in my face, flapping around my head, and I lift my hands, batting them away as they chop at my skin. I try to scream at the pain as they cut into me but my voice is empty, and as I watch the pages they slow and stop in mid-air, turning around and folding themselves into cranes, just as I made for Keiko.

Their wings flap and they fly around my head in circles, yet as quickly as the wind came, it disappears again, scattering the cranes across the city, and I'm left in total quietness and utterly alone.

You have no one now, I hear in my mind. *You failed everyone.*

I think of the doctor, and how many patients he had and how little time. I take one last look over the city of so many injured, where my life was and my hopes were.

'I will make it one fewer,' I say. 'More time and chance for those who deserve it. I make this sacrifice for them.'

Pulling in one final breath, I close my eyes and lean forward. For a moment, I feel the air against my skin, and then I feel nothing at all.

Gentle chatter.

A soft beeping.

Wheels across a hard floor.

I hear sounds first.

The click of a door.

A rustle of paper.

'He's waking.' A woman's voice, an unfamiliar accent.

My eyelids flutter against the whiteness, blinking

into focus on a shape in front of them. A round face appears, dark hair, brown eyes, a slow smile.

'Who are you?' my voice croaks.

'I work here.'

My vision floats around the room: white beds, white ceiling, white walls, white pillows.

'Where am I?'

'A hospital in Tokyo,' she says.

I close my eyes, open them again, yet everything still looks the same. I sigh and shake my head.

'I don't understand,' I say. 'How did I get here? Why am I here?'

'You were brought here from Hiroshima.'

'But –'

'You were in the Red Cross Hospital. You were in a very bad way . . .'

'No,' I say.

'It's not surprising you don't remember . . .'

'No . . .' I try to think . . . to remember . . . the white . . . the bomb . . . heat . . . we found Keiko . . . Hiro died . . . walked to the hospital . . . abandoned Keiko . . .

Keiko, I think.

I drag my legs around the side of the bed and haul myself to sitting. My body hurts and my head pounds, yet I pull the sheet from me.

'I have to go,' I say.

She shakes her head. 'No, you can't,' she replies.

A strong hand rests on my arm, and I notice for the first time that there are bandages on my arms and legs and wires coming from me.

'I have to.' I rest my feet on the floor, but as I ease myself to standing I turn dizzy and her hands are on mine. Her face swims before me as the bed comes back up to me and again I'm lying down.

'You're simply not well enough to go anywhere,' she says.

'I have to go back to Hiroshima,' I say. 'I have to. You don't understand. She'll be waiting for me. I told her to. Told her I'd come back for her.' My throat hurts as I talk, and even though I've barely been awake for five minutes, I am so intolerably tired.

'Please, help me up. I have to go.'

'Who'll be waiting for you?' she asks.

'Keiko.' Her name sounds strange in the quiet of the ward. 'I couldn't carry her any further. I went on to get help, but . . . I left her by herself. Next to a burnt-out tram. I went to get help. I couldn't carry her any more. I tried . . .'

'When was that?' she asks. 'The day of the bomb?'

'The day after.'

Her eyes blink far too much, and she looks away from me towards the door, around the ward and back again. She tries to smile but there is pity behind it. 'I don't think she'll be there any more,' she says softly. 'That was . . . a while ago . . .'

I stare at her. 'How long?'

'I think I should get a doctor,' she says. 'I should tell someone you're awake.'

'How long?' I ask again.

'I don't know the exact date you arrived here.'

'But you know what the date is now!'

'I really don't –'

'How long?' I shout.

'Since the bomb?' she says quietly. 'Four weeks.'

'Four weeks?' I repeat. 'It's September?'

She nods. 'September the third.'

Four weeks? I think. Four weeks since I left Keiko on the way to the hospital. I can see her still, her eyes looking into mine as I passed her the crane. The promise I made to her . . .

'No.' I shake my head. 'No, that cannot be right . . . no . . .'

'I'm sorry,' she says. 'Truly I am.'

My head is heavy and drops to my hands. My eyes sting. My chest is tight. I can't breathe. My face burns.

The words I said to Hiro come back, the promise I made to Keiko, and I see her in my mind, sitting alone at the tram as darkness creeps over her, smothering her as she waits for me. In vain.

When did she give up on me?

What did she do?

Did she move? Try to stay alive? Or did she fade away as she watched for my return?

'I'm sorry, Keiko,' I whisper to the air. 'I'm so, so sorry.'

This time I don't even turn to hide my face as the tears fall, and as they fall so does darkness.

I wake again much later.

It's dusk outside my window.

Flashes of memories leap unbidden into my head – a doctor holding water for me, a red tomato, leaving the hospital – yes, I remember leaving the hospital – looking for the tramlines . . . but where . . . where . . . ?

In hospital . . . the open window – yes, I remember that too now – climbing through the window, sitting on the ledge, leaning out . . . but . . . how can that be . . . ?

I picture the hospital in my mind.

Its windows aren't like that, I think. *Big, yes, but made up of many small panes. It would not be possible to climb through.*

And the flying pages? The cranes?

You dreamed it, I tell myself. *Imagined it.*

Hallucinations or wishful thinking. You did not try to kill yourself. This is reality. Four weeks is reality.

The woman is at my bedside again.

'Tell me you are real,' I say.

I watch her lips tilt up into a smile and her eyes crinkle. 'I'm real,' she says. 'Did you think you were dreaming?'

I don't reply. *No*, I think, *I thought I was dead. Hoped I was.*

'Are you a nurse?' I ask.

She shakes her head. 'A translator,' she says. 'I'm here to help the doctors.'

I frown. 'Why do they need a translator? Where are they from?'

She pauses. 'Do you remember anything since the bomb?' she asks eventually. 'Anything between then and now? The doctors tell me you regained consciousness a few times.'

'I don't remember a thing,' I say.

She sighs. 'You should eat,' she says, and she puts a bowl of rice in front of me with some chopsticks, again I notice the strange lilt of her words.

'Where are you from?' I ask. 'The same place as the doctors?'

There's a pause again in her voice, worry on her brow. 'I'm from Portland in Oregon,' she says.

'You're an American?' My voice lifts with incredulity.

'That I am,' she replies.

'And . . . and the doctors?' I ask.

'Some are American,' she replies. 'Not all.'

'But . . .' I frown because I don't understand. 'What . . . what are American doctors doing here?'

She lifts the jug and pours water into a glass. 'A lot has happened since the atomic bomb,' she says.

'Atomic bomb? It wasn't petrol? Or a cluster bomb?'

'No,' she says. 'It was an atomic bomb.'

I stare at her.

'The Americans dropped it.' Her voice is quiet. 'One on Nagasaki as well, three days later.'

I do not say a word.

'I'm sorry,' she says, and there is genuine sadness in her voice. 'American troops came over after Japan surrendered –'

'Japan surrendered? No, surely that cannot be true. The Emperor, he would never surrender. You are wrong. That would never happen!' My voice is loud, other patients are staring at me, a nurse looks through the door, a doctor approaches, but the woman shakes her head at him.

'Please, try to stay calm –'

'The Emperor would never surrender. It cannot be true . . .'

'Please . . .'

I look from her to the other patients around the room with their heads bowed, to the doctor standing nearby, and I remember the bomb, the heat, the fires, the destruction, the bodies, and I imagine more of the same in Nagasaki. But to surrender? I feel cheated, deceived, ashamed of our army.

'The doctor over there,' I say, 'is he American?'

'Yes, that's Dr Edwards of the American Army

Corps. He's been looking after you. I'm in the Women's Army Corps. I trained in Iowa. My father is Japanese. He went to live in America in 1912 and met my mother there. I've always spoken both languages.'

'Japan is occupied by Americans,' I murmur, shocked that such words are coming from my mouth and seem true, and I think of the dismay that would be on my father's face. He would kill himself before surrendering, as would many, but . . . and again I think of the bomb, and with a sickening horror I remember rumours of the terror inflicted by our own troops during battle.

'Are you here for revenge?' I ask. 'To laugh at us now we have been conquered?'

She shakes her head. 'No. Why would anyone do that? No. We're here to help you rebuild, and to do some studies of the bomb.'

'Then that is what I am? A study?'

'I suppose in a way you are,' she says. 'Only a few of the worst affected were brought here. Nobody understands the full effects of the bomb yet. But you have been looked after very well. If you hadn't been brought here . . .'

She passes me the water. I take my time drinking it and the ward falls silent.

'Who was she?' Her voice is quiet and calm. 'The girl you mentioned earlier. The one you made a promise to. Was she your girlfriend?'

I stare into the cup of water, watching the ripples across the surface. 'My friend's sister,' I say. 'She was five years old.'

I think of Keiko's five short years, and the lifetime of guilt stretching ahead of me.

This is not an honourable way to live.

'Y'know,' the woman says, 'she may still be alive. Somebody could've helped her. She could be in one of the orphanages. You don't know that she didn't make it.'

I can't reply.

'My father had this expression,' she continues. 'When I'd say my school work was too hard, or I couldn't learn to ride my bike – "You're a three-day monk," he'd say to me. You know that expression?'

'It means you give up too easily,' I reply.

She nods.

'You think I gave up too easily when I left her? You think –'

'No, no, no,' she says. 'Not at all. How could I say that when I wasn't there? No, I mean you're giving up too easily on her now.'

Her words are too kind for me.

She reaches forward and lifts something from the table next to my bed.

'I think this is yours,' she says. 'Quite a book. It looks like lots of pages!'

I spin around. 'How . . . ?'

'It was in the pocket of the gown you were wearing.'

I stare at it in her hands.

'It's very difficult to read,' she says. 'It must've got wet. Some of the pages are stiff, and the covers are swollen. Did you tape the volumes together?'

I nod as I take it from her, and I brush my fingers down the spines and over the edges of the paper.

'My father gave it to me,' I whisper.

'Well, I hope you've read the first page,' she says, 'because someone's ripped it out.'

My hand is over my mouth; I cannot say a word. Cannot believe *The Tale of Genji* has made it all this way with me.

'I have to go,' she says. 'I'll come and see you tomorrow.' She stands and walks towards the door.

'What is your name?' I manage to say after her.

She turns around and smiles. 'Megumi,' she replies.

The doctors are kind. The nurses too. Their tender hands touch my burns and wounds with the care of a parent or loved one, yet still the pain washes through me when they peel off the bandages, and I lie with my thoughts in some other place to distract myself from their shaking heads and clicking tongues.

I am not healing, it seems.

After their rounds are finished, they leave me

with a pile of newspapers, all dated after the bomb, and I read them, one after another after another, into the night and the early hours of the morning.

I learn of the bomb on Nagasaki, the surrender of our Emperor, the occupation of our land by our enemy. I learn little of the effects of the bomb save for burns, but much about the confusion of the doctors who treat them and how death comes to those who seem uninjured as quickly and as unexpectedly as nightmares come to the sleeping.

As I read more and more, I realise I am neither angry nor resentful, and I will make no judgements and take no sides, for it is done. All I see now is that too many have suffered.

I stop reading only when complaints from my fellow patients mean my small light must be turned out, yet my guilt continues even as sleep claims me, for in my dreams, every night, visions of Keiko come to me.

Megumi returns the following day. She passes me a cup of tea and I cradle it in my hands.

At the bed opposite an elderly woman is feeding rice to a middle-aged man and I watch the care with which she lifts the chopsticks to his mouth and waits for him to eat. Such patience she has.

'You have no family, Ichiro?' Megumi asks.

'My father went away to fight five years ago. We haven't heard from him in three. My mother would've been at work when the bomb hit. She would not have had any shelter.'

Her silence is her reply.

'Do you believe the dead come to us in dreams?' I ask.

'Like ghosts?' she replies.

I nod as I lift the cup to my lips.

'I believe in heaven and hell, and that if you are good you go to heaven. I believe that God created the earth. But I don't believe in ghosts.'

'Many people claim to have seen ghosts. My mother said she woke one morning to see my father at the foot of her bed, his uniform red with blood.'

'Maybe it was only what she was afraid of. Her imagination playing tricks on her.'

I take another sip of tea.

'Tell me about Keiko,' she says.

After twenty minutes I'm exhausted by the retelling of my ineptitude and guilt. I want to sleep.

Yet I can smell the cleanliness of her uniform, the perfume in her hair, and I look up to see her brown eyes close to me, a flick of hair curling by her ear.

'I know some people stationed near Hiroshima,' she whispers. 'I could ask them if they can help. Perhaps if they go into the city they could ask around,' she says.

I only nod my reply for I cannot speak; my heart is so full with gratitude.

Time in hospital passes as if minutes were days.

I read the crinkled pages of my book, but am yet to find the magic my father spoke of.

I want to leave but am not allowed, and while I contemplate discharging myself against doctors' orders, I fear I have not the strength to care for myself, and haven't yet worked out where I shall live.

I do not know if Hiroshima holds anything but memories for me now.

Keiko continues to visit me every night.

Sometimes the dreams are memories of her before that day: playing in the garden, chatting with her mother, chasing Hiro around the house as he pretended he could not outrun her.

'Are you lonely sometimes?' she once asked as we shared a table. She was drawing a picture, Hiro and I were discussing homework.

'Why?' I asked.

'There is only you. I'd be lonely without Hiro.'

'I wouldn't be lonely without you,' Hiro replied. 'I'd be able to eat all the *dorayaki* pancakes Mother makes, and not have to look after you while she's at work!'

She glared at him, but as Hiro looked back down to his work I leaned over and whispered in her ear, 'Without you, I would be lonely.'

She looked at me with eyes of wonderment and I winked at her.

Mostly, though, the dreams are of her on that day, distorted by my guilt and imagination into nightmares.

Her face as I passed her the crane and stood to leave. Her eyes as I promised I would return.

'You didn't come back,' she says. 'You lied.'

I feel her weight in my arms and her hair on my face.

'I was so tired,' I tell her. 'We would not have made it together. I didn't know what else to do.'

'You abandoned me,' she says.

I try to remember how I felt, the pain in my limbs and in my face, and the exhaustion, yet I cannot.

You can't have felt that bad, a voice in my mind says.

Can't have been that ill, or injured.

Could've carried on.

Could've rescued her.

Saved her.

In my head I scream back:

I know! I know!

I dream of Hiro too.

Sitting next to each other at elementary school. Sharing food if either of us forgot our lunch. Walking home, complaining of teachers and homework, nagging parents and household chores.

And of his face in the water, his eyes as I spoke the last words he would ever hear. A promise I could never fulfil.

Night after night I wake from these nightmares

into the dark and quiet of the hospital, the window luring me to jump from it, or the door to run through it.

Why did I survive if not to save her? I think.

Megumi comes by often. I start to recognise the sound of her feet across the floor.

'No news yet,' she says, as my expectant eyes lift to meet hers and I live for the day her feet will move quicker and her face will be lit by a smile and her head will nod.

The man in the bed next to me, who was about to be discharged, develops a red rash overnight that covers his entire body; two days later he is dead.

A few days will pass where it seems I am not ill at all, only for the next to see me unable to stay awake for more than half an hour or barely able to even move a limb.

My wounds are plagued with infections and are slow to heal.

'Why?' I ask the doctors again and again. 'Because of the bomb?'

They only shrug.

Thoughts of Hiroshima are incessant. How many were killed? How many survived? What did they do with the dead? Where are the survivors living? Are they rebuilding? What will happen to where my house stood?

Questions fill my head, driving me to distraction.

On and on.

Megumi tries to answer them, but more often than not she doesn't know and will rub a hand over her tired face as she apologises.

She brings me American novels, sits at my bedside and reads to me, translating as she goes, and as her voice lifts me to lavish parties with jazz music, or California fields with migrant workers, or down the backstreets of Los Angeles with a detective, the air is filled with the magic my father spoke of.

Yet I am impatient with myself.

I want to be well and I want to leave.

I want to find Keiko.

I have been feeling well for a few days when I hear her feet moving faster along the corridor, and it is with strength I have been missing for a long time that I pull myself to sitting and wait for her face of sunshine to appear around the corner, with her crisp uniform and her hair tied back.

Yet surprise fills me as she stands in the doorway, a jacket around her shoulders and a bag in her hand.

'We're going out,' she says. 'The doctor says you are well enough. We're taking a trip. To Hiroshima.'

'Do you have news?' I ask.

'Not really,' she says. 'Just advice on where to look.' She shrugs. 'Maybe a lead.'

For weeks I've been waiting for this. It is with great effort now that I control my breathing and keep my face still from emotion, but my legs are already out of the bed.

She is at my side.

'Here,' she says. 'I have some clothes. I hope they're your size. The male soldiers sent them.'

'American clothes?' I ask.

She nods and places them on the bed next to me.

A pair of grey trousers, a blue shirt and a sweater. I rest my hand on them. Soft. Clean. Ironed.

'They bought you new underwear,' she whispers, and passes me a brown paper bag.

'Why?' I ask.

'To help. Because they know what it's like to lose someone. Because they have young sisters. Because you – we – are not enemies.'

The ward is quiet, yet so are our voices. I lift the clothes from the bed.

'You must tell them I send my gratitude,' I whisper.

The train journey from Tokyo to Hiroshima is a long one, nearly a whole day, and the time I do not spend sleeping I spend staring out of the window at towns and villages I have never seen before.

'How was I taken to Tokyo?' I ask Megumi.

'Some people were brought in on trains like this,' she says.

'The train lines were working?'

She nods.

I watch the soft green fields, the tree-lined hills, the tiny roads and isolated houses go by, and I wonder what Hiroshima is like now.

My memories of how it was before that day are clear; the wide T-shape of the Aioi-bashi Bridge, the metal bird statues on the Yenko Bridge, the low boats on the Motoyasu River, the metal or wooden trams clattering along the lines, the fancy dome of the Industrial Promotion Hall, the hustle and bustle of the streets.

'It was the first time Hiro and I had a day off together,' I say, still staring out of the window. 'If it had been the day before, or the day after, we would have been inside the factory, making aeroplane parts. Someone asked if I would swap my day off. If I had not agreed, then I wouldn't have taken him into that river. He could still be alive.'

'What is the phrase?' Megumi asks. '*Shikata ga nai?*'

Through the window I fix my eyes to the distance and watch the colours of the fields, the roads, the houses, the flowers and the trees as they blur and merge into one.

'*Shikata ga nai?*' I say. Oh well? 'How can you be so flippant with someone's life?'

'Decisions were made that you have to live with. You led him into the river to save him from the fire. It was your only option. You didn't kill him. In fact, if it wasn't for changing your day off, you'd be dead. Then where would Keiko be?'

We are silent. I have no words, and so say

nothing, yet between us pass a million things in the space of a second, and at that precise moment, I realise what I feel for her.

I look away, for while it is brilliant, it is also intolerable.

A flutter of nervous conversation follows between us about nothing more than the uncomfortableness of trains and the impracticality of large newspapers, and shortly after I drift into a sleep where dreams place me in a sea buffeted by waves.

She has brought food and drink, and when I awake she takes out containers of rice and fish and passes them to me with chopsticks and a napkin.

'The hospital provided this,' she explains.

'Who paid for the train?' I ask.

She swallows her food. 'A few of us.'

'I shall repay you.'

She shakes her head. 'No,' she says. 'It's a gift.'

'That is very kind,' I whisper. 'But I cannot accept.'

'Why?' she asks. 'Because we're American?'

'No.'

'Because we're your enemy?'

'You are not my enemy; you are . . .'

'Then because you're too proud?' She smiles.

I shake my head and lower my eyes. 'Because I do not deserve it,' I murmur.

I hear her intake of breath. 'Don't you deserve to be happy?' she asks.

I do not reply.

'To live a good life? Have a future? Maybe if you can find Keiko, you can move on.'

'I do not deserve any of it,' I say. 'I failed her and my best friend. How can I live with that? He died so that I could save her, and yet I didn't!'

'You did your best,' she says.

'No,' I say. 'I should not have left her. I should have carried on.'

'If you'd carried on, you would never have made it to the hospital. You would both be dead now. You did what was best at the time. You gave both of you a chance. It was the only thing you could've done.'

She leans closer. 'Maybe the doctor you spoke

to went back to find her, or sent someone to her. Maybe someone else found her and looked after her. You don't know. But you owe it to her, and Hiro, not to give up. Find her if you can. If you can't, you must carry her memory with you, but if you die, or give up, who is there to remember? Either way,' she says, '*shikata ga nai*. It's about time you stopped feeling sorry for yourself.'

I put a piece of fish in my mouth and chew, and after I swallow I look up at her.

'Tell me about home,' I say.

The conversation lifts into funny anecdotes and happy memories of her life growing up in Oregon, how her father came to live in America, and of her younger brother who writes to her all the time and sends photographs that fill her with guilt for not being homesick.

'I love Japan,' she says. 'I'd like to see more of it, but . . .'

'I've never been out of Hiroshima before,' I tell her, and we share dreams about seeing Mount Fuji, photographing storks in the wild, and visiting Shinto shrines.

'We sound like tourists,' she says with a smile.

Time with her passes with ease and with comfort, yet while my heart longs to smile, my body and face remain stiff and unemotional, and for daring any happiness to come to me, I am still plagued with guilt.

The landscape and the mood changes.

Rice fields are no longer lush and green but scarred with streaks of brown, and houses slump as if in pain, with broken windows and falling roof tiles.

Then, as if a line has been drawn, the houses are all but gone.

From the hills behind us to the sea a few miles

out stretches a graveyard of a city; the occasional concrete buildings like weather-worn gravestones stand among crushed rubble, charred trees without leaves and scorched telegraph poles.

The train slows as we take it in.

'One bomb,' I say.

Next to me, Megumi is silent.

'I do not recognise my own home.'

We step off the train at Hiroshima station.

Although the carcass of the station building remains, it is little more than that. The ceiling is on the floor, the windows are empty, and rubble lies like mountains waiting to be conquered. Yet the tracks are clear, the trains are running and the platform is packed with people.

'What are they all doing here?' I ask Megumi.

'Looking for someone?' she suggests with a shrug. 'A friend or relative, maybe?'

I stop, but crowds of bodies still walk towards

me, part around me and re-form beyond me, as if I am a rock in a river.

'Their faces are so blank,' she says.

'They are preoccupied with their task,' I say. 'They have no time for emotion, although it is there beneath the surface.'

From the station we cross the river and head south.

We walk down cleared streets, winding through the desolation as if our brains have been disconnected and our feet take us at their will. Rubble is piled at the sides, and among it shanties for the homeless have been built from tin or wood, and outside them steam rises from make-do stoves. Washing stretches over skeletal branches of trees.

At my side a man pulls a wooden cart, its large wheels clattering as they hit holes in the road and on the back of it sits a boy with burns down his legs.

I want to ask them where they are going and where they have been.

Where they were when the bomb hit.

How they survived.

How they are living now, and where.

If they have seen a young girl, holding a paper crane made out of a page of a book.

But they are silent and I let them be.

'Where are we going?' I ask Megumi.

She pulls a piece of paper from her pocket. 'My contacts gave me a list of places to try,' she says. 'But I don't know where any of them are.' She hands the paper to me.

'Fukuromachi Elementary School,' I read. 'Oshiba Elementary School.'

'They're temporary hospitals now,' she explains.

Reading down the list, I nod as I think about where these places are in relation to each other.

'Hijiyama School . . .'

'That one's a shelter for orphans,' she says.

'We'll go there first,' I say. 'Do you have my book?'

She nods as she pats her bag.

Using remnants of buildings and tramlines to guide us towards the Kyobashi River and the Hijiyama School, we turn and head east.

In the distance and to our right is the tower of the Red Cross Hospital and I fight back memories that will serve no use today, and I fight back whatever it is that is telling me Keiko walks again at my side.

I will not look down, for she is not there.

As we cross the river I hear the water underneath splashing against the bank and the concrete legs of the bridge.

'Look! There's a rowing boat in the water,' Megumi says. 'Children are playing in it.'

I hear the dip and pull of the oars and breathe deep to keep the memories at bay.

We find the Hijiyama School without much difficulty, for it is one of the few buildings standing and people are keen to help.

Children play nearby, some throwing a ball to each other, a couple sitting on a length of wood made into a see-saw, another climbing piles of rubble and jumping the ravine between them. We approach one boy sitting quietly on a concrete wall.

'Hello,' I say.

He jumps in surprise as if he didn't see us, yet bows forward in respect.

'I'm looking for someone,' I tell him. 'Her name is Keiko Matsuya.'

He shakes his head.

'She's my friend's sister. She's about this tall.' I place my hand near the top of my leg. 'Her hair is cut at her chin.'

He shakes his head again, still not looking up.

'She has a round face and . . . Are you listening to me?' I snap.

His head shoots up but it misses my direction, focusing somewhere behind my left shoulder.

'My apologies,' he says.

I stare at him. 'No,' I say. 'It is me who should be apologising. What happened to your eyes?'

'I looked straight at the *pika*,' he says. 'They're burnt.'

He leaps down from the wall and, tapping a skinny branch of a tree across the ground, walks towards us.

'Everyone comes here looking for someone,' he says. 'One day my father will return from the war and come looking for me too.'

'I'm sure he'll return a hero,' I tell him.

A smile stretches across his face. 'And he will be proud I have survived!' he says.

'He will.' I nod.

But the smile slips from his face and he cocks his head to one side as his brow furrows. 'I have been here since it opened,' he says. 'I have not heard of anyone called Keiko, and I hear well.'

'Do you remember well?' I ask him.

'Like the Emperor himself, sensei.'

His use of sensei – sir – brings a smile to my face, for I wonder how old he imagines I am. 'Good. Will you remember her name?'

'Keiko Matsuya,' he says.

'Excellent. Well, if you see her, I want you to give her this.' Megumi passes my book from her bag, and with my pen I scrawl 'Keiko' down the margin, my name next to it and 'Tokyo Hospital'.

The boy frowns as he hears the sound of the page ripping, yet he waits patiently as I fold it.

I place the paper crane in his hand. His fingers feel along the bird's wings.

'You need a thousand, sensei, to get your wish.'

'If I have to fold a thousand cranes and take them to a thousand places to find her, then that I will do.'

'She must be very special.'

'To me she is,' I whisper. 'Just as I'm certain you are to others.'

He turns and walks away, his tree branch

scratching the path in front of him, and I wonder if anyone has told him the war is over.

At each school, home, shelter or hospital we visit I leave a paper crane, each with her name and mine and the hospital written on the edge.

At one school, messages for the missing are scrawled up the walls, and I add one from me to Keiko, and on the floor next to it I leave a crane.

Pages of my book are disappearing to wishes for her return.

Time is lost to walking.

The sun is setting on a long and difficult day and we have only the Red Cross Hospital to go.

Exhaustion pulls at me. I veer west so I can walk along the tramlines again, as I did with Keiko, yet I know she won't be there.

But the burnt-out tram where I left her is, and at that precise spot I sit down. There is nothing to mark this as anything but a tram destroyed by an atomic bomb.

Megumi sits next to me. 'Is this where . . . ?'

'Where I left her? Yes.'

'I didn't mean it that way –'

I raise a hand to quieten her. 'I know,' I whisper.

Across the darkness I watch the flicker of the fires among the ruins, people cooking or keeping warm. Alive.

'Ichiro, it's perfectly possible that someone helped her, or that she took herself somewhere, and took the crane with her, and that she is still alive,' she continues.

'Unlikely,' I say. 'Although, admittedly, possible.'

I turn to look at her. My face is unmoving and my eyes will not water, yet hers glisten and in them flicker the erratic lights of a city in pain. She rests a hand on mine and everything around us is quiet.

In our own silences, we hear each other.

Megumi stands and offers me her hand.

We continue, Megumi at my side, her arm in mine to keep me upright.

The hospital gates are open and welcoming. The paths are clear now and a white flag with a solid red cross hangs from the windows of the central rectangular tower.

'Do you remember the name of the doctor you spoke to?' Megumi asks as we step up to the main doors. 'The one who gave you the water.'

I shake my head. 'I only remember what he looked like.'

Through the doors we find a young woman at a desk. She's surrounded by patients sitting in chairs or on the floor, leaning against walls or wobbly tables, but as we approach she stands, smiles and bows.

'I am looking for someone,' I say. 'A young girl, five years old, her name is Keiko Matsuya.'

Sitting again, she flicks through papers on her desk.

'I don't know if she is here. I don't know where she is,' I say.

The young woman stops and looks up at me. 'I'm sorry.' Her voice quietens and her face softens. 'Many, many people are missing. We may never find them or know –'

'Please,' I say, lifting a hand. 'Can I take a moment of your time to explain?'

She listens to my story, and although she appears sympathetic I know she will have heard a million other stories, many sadder, more painful or more upsetting to care much for mine.

As I finish, she hands me a cup of water.

'At the time of the bombing, there were three hundred doctors in Hiroshima. Two hundred and seventy of those were killed so it is not surprising to hear the reaction of the staff you spoke to. I can only imagine how difficult it must've been for them to have to refuse you, and your pain on hearing that.' She sucks in a deep breath.

'I'm afraid,' she continues, 'that the doctor you describe sounds like Dr Yamamoto. He died last week.'

I recoil from her, grabbing the desk to steady myself. 'No,' I breathe. 'But . . . of what? He said he was the least injured.'

She sighs. 'We don't know. It's happened a lot. People who weren't injured by the bomb and appeared quite healthy suddenly become ill.' She turns away from the waiting patients and lowers her voice. 'They complain of a debilitating fatigue,' she says. 'In many cases they develop rashes on the skin, and then they simply fade away.'

I nod, blinking and blinking my eyes, trying to ignore how tired I am.

'Even if your Keiko survived, I'm afraid . . .' Her voice peters away.

'Can we look around?' I ask. 'I'd like to check.'

She nods. 'Of course.'

The hospital is no longer the vision of hell it was that night, yet still the windows are broken, and although plastic sheeting is nailed over to offer some protection, the wind flaps it too loudly for the peace these patients need, and any rain would pour in the sides.

And still it is crowded.

In the corridors, every chair is filled with someone waiting for treatment or medicines. In the wards, every bed I step between is occupied and every face stares at me with hope that I could be a lost relative or friend, only to look away with disappointment when they realise I am not.

Most are adults, but when I see a body the size of a child, something inside me lifts, only to fall when the head turns to reveal a face that is not Keiko.

She is not in the first ward we try, and nor is she in the last.

She is not in any of the chairs or at any of the tables.

Nor is she strolling down any of the corridors or talking to any of the nurses or staring out of any of the broken windows.

'We should find somewhere to rest for the night,' Megumi whispers.

I don't reply, but as she turns, I follow her.

We had thought finding somewhere to spend the night would be easy, but I'm too tired to walk back to any of the American bases, and of course there are barely houses, let alone hostels.

All the wards are full, and the waiting areas too, so we step out into the dark and around the back of the hospital, following the narrow paths cleared of debris, and looking for some kind of room or shelter.

To the side, tucked away and hardly visible, is a small doorway. Pushing the door open, we call a greeting, but there is no reply.

Together we step inside, hands extended to feel through the darkness.

'It's dry,' she says, 'and sheltered.'

I feel ashamed – she is a visitor in my country. I should be able to offer her comfort, yet there is nothing I can provide.

In the corner we find some old tatami mats and sheeting, and although the dust from them is thick in our throats, we spread some on the floor and pull the rest over ourselves.

I listen to the sounds of the night – the hoot of an owl, the scurry of a rat, the crackle of distant fires keeping families warm. A distant cry.

Where are you, Keiko? I think. *Are you still alive? Come to me in my dreams and lead me to you.*

Yet I know it is futile; in the morning I must return to Tokyo.

The rustle of Megumi's covers breaks the silence, and I'm struck by how odd it is that it is only now I realise we should not be sharing the same room.

'Megumi?' I whisper. 'I am sorry. I should not be in here with you. That was disrespectful of me. I will go right away.'

'Don't be silly,' she says. 'You're not going anywhere.'

The darkness is so complete in this little room that I cannot see anything, yet I hear her moving again and the drag of her mat across the floor.

'Thank you for coming with me,' I say, sensing her close.

'It was my pleasure,' she replies. 'I'm sorry we didn't find her.'

I don't answer.

'One day,' she says, and her warm hands rest on mine.

'I should stay,' I say to Megumi as we walk across the city the next morning. 'There are so many more places I should look.'

She shakes her head and I see her eyes wandering over the injuries on my face and the frown it brings to her.

'You should go back to the hospital,' she says. 'We can return. Maybe when the city is more settled. School will begin again, and Keiko is only five; she will have to go to school. We can write to them all, or telephone.'

I walk on with her towards the station.

'I will return,' I tell her.

'And I will come with you,' she replies.

Through the train window I watch Hiroshima disappear from me, imagining that somewhere among the rubble and ruins, the shacks and the makeshift homes in anything that offers shelter, is Keiko, waiting for me.

Maybe before I can come back again she will have cause to go to the Red Cross Hospital.

Maybe she will see the crane on the front desk,

my name and hers down the edge, the words 'Tokyo Hospital'.

Maybe the nurse will tell Keiko I left it for her, that she promised to look after it until the day came.

Keiko will smile. 'He promised me he'd come back,' she'll say to the nurse. 'And he did.'

It isn't until we are pulling into Tokyo Station and Megumi is gently saying my name that I wake, and I follow her, blurry-eyed, from the train, across the station and into a taxi.

I remember sitting in it, but I remember nothing more until I wake back in my bed the following day.

Dr Edwards is watching me as I open my eyes, Megumi next to him.

'How was Hiroshima?' he asks through her.

'Bleak,' I answer.

'They say nothing will grow there for seventy-five years.'

'That's not true,' I reply. 'We saw new shoots

of green pushing up through the earth. People are preparing vegetable patches in front of homes they've built. Have you not seen any photographs?'

He shakes his head. 'Rumours upon rumours,' he says, and he drums his fingers across his cheek as he does when he is thinking. 'We have a few more *hibakusha* here – you know that phrase?'

'Yes,' I reply. 'It means "bomb-affected person", not "survivor".'

'That's right. Well, you're not the only patient of mine who is a *hibakusha*. Neither are you the first to take a trip back there.'

He sucks in a deep breath and looks at me. 'There's a curious thing which cannot be coincidence.'

I try to sit up more, but my body aches as if I've tumbled down a hillside. I grimace and the skin on my face pulls across my burns.

Megumi helps me.

'Each one of you who's visited Hiroshima has returned here in a worse state than when they left,' he continues, pausing as Megumi translates. 'Tired to the point of exhaustion, bleeding that is near impossible to stop, wounds that had been healing suddenly open again, and some with red spots on their skin.' He pauses and lowers his eyes.

'Those with the spots,' I whisper, 'did they die?'

He looks into my eyes and nods.

'A woman in Hiroshima said the same thing,' I say.

I look down at my own arms; they look clear. I want to lift up my top, check my stomach, take off my clothes, check the rest of me. 'Doctor . . .' I say.

He shakes his head, guessing my question. 'No,' he says, 'but what I'm trying to say is . . . we can get you back to how you were before your visit, I hope. We can look after you and build you up, but you can't go back to Hiroshima again.'

'But –'

'Not for now. Not if you want to be well.' His fingers tap at his cheek again. 'We're still learning,' he says, his voice low and deep. 'At the moment we think there's something left in the air that's making people ill, but we're only starting to understand. What we do know is that every single *hibakusha* who's returned, even for a day, has come back very ill. My advice to you has to be not to return.'

'I can't go back to live there?'

He sighs as he looks from me to Megumi and to the floor. 'I certainly wouldn't advise it.'

'What about the people who are in hospitals there?'

'What can I say? Maybe they'd get better if they moved away. I don't know. I only know what I've seen and what other doctors have told me. My patients are my concern, and so my advice to you, and to the others, is not to go back. Not yet.'

'I have nowhere else to live.'

'You still have a home in Hiroshima?' he asks.

I sigh and shake my head. 'I have the land where my home stood.'

'Like many,' he says. He continues talking to Megumi, but I'm drifting away from the conversation.

The bomb has changed everything.

I think back to my room: my futon, my desk with books across it, the view from my window. Sitting at the breakfast table while my mother cooks, the glorious smell, her smile as she turns to me. The creak of the front door as I head out to school or to our mobilisation, the sunlight flickering through the branches of the mimosa tree, Hiro waiting for me at the corner, Keiko in tow to take to kindergarten.

Gone.

I glance back up to see Dr Edwards smiling at me. 'I'll leave you for now,' he says, and bows his goodbyes.

Megumi stays though, and sits next to my bed with her hands folded in her lap. 'Ichiro,' she says, 'how are you feeling?'

'Better for sleeping,' I reply. 'Thank you for taking care of me.'

She smiles, but it falls from her too quickly. 'I have something to tell you – not about Keiko, about me.'

The ward is quiet; patients are reading or sleeping, concentrating on a puzzle or staring into space. Megumi shuffles closer.

'You know who General MacArthur is?' she asks.

'Of course, he's the American commander.' I lower my voice. 'He's in charge of Japan now.'

Her hands twist together as she talks. 'He doesn't approve of enlisted women serving overseas.'

'What does that mean, he doesn't approve? Does that matter?'

She nods. 'Yes. It means if I want to remain in the army corps, I have to go back to the States.'

My chest turns hot. 'You have to leave Japan?'

'Or if I want to stay here in Tokyo, I can apply to work for the civil service, as a civilian.'

I want to tell her not to go. To forget the army corps. That I want to be with her. But I cannot speak. I'm struck by this heat in my chest and overwhelmed with sadness that she could be leaving.

'I applied for the civil service,' she says. 'Last week.'

'And?' I ask, managing to keep my face still and calm and my voice level.

'They said yes.'

I breathe out, louder and heavier than I mean to.

'But only for a year. Then I have to go home. And I have to tell you –' she glances up at me, but too quickly away again – 'that I'm not going to be working here any more.' Now she stares into my eyes. 'I won't see you as much . . . I won't be able to drop in for a cup of tea and to read with you.'

'But you'll still be in Japan? In Tokyo?' I ask.

She nods. 'And if you want me to, I can still visit you. I'd like to. If you'd like that.'

Relief spills over me and I cannot help but smile. 'If I'd like that?' I say.

She nods.

'If I'd like that?' I repeat.

I look into her face and I am filled with warmth. 'Yes,' I say. 'Yes, I would like that.'

'All right,' she says.

'Every day?' I ask.

Again she nods, and she smiles a smile that lights up the room and my whole world.

'Every day,' she says. 'For a year, every day.'

In the 'before', my life was planned out.

I was to be an engineer. My father would return from war a hero. My mother would be happy. Hiro and I would be lifelong friends. We would go to each other's weddings, celebrate the births of our children, be invited to each other's houses. We wouldn't leave Hiroshima because there would be no need, but we would travel with our families and come back with stories of things we'd seen and done, and photographs to share.

Every time we would meet up he would tell me stories of his younger sister, Keiko, and what she was doing. He would tell me that she said hello and thanked me for taking her to kindergarten on all those mornings when their mother had to work.

Sometimes, on special occasions, I would see her and marvel at how much she'd grown and what a young lady she had become.

In the morning it will be a year since that day.

A year since I last saw Keiko.

A flash of light set a new course for everything.

Today we will travel to Hiroshima by train, Megumi and me, for the first time since she accompanied me while I was still a patient.

Circumstance and ill health have prevented us from visiting sooner, yet all that time, since I was discharged and moved to a room in Megumi's building, found a part-time job and began studying again, I have written to countless schools, aid organisations, hospitals, orphanages, shelters, inquiring after Keiko, including in each a crane folded from a page of my book, with both our names and my new address written down the edge.

A letter is too easy to ignore, forget or put in a bin. A paper crane is a curious thing. People sense an attachment and will leave it on a table or a sill. Others will notice it and take a closer look at it, the typed words along with my scrawl tempting eyes to read and remember.

I left one at the hospital too. Dr Edwards promised it would stay where it could be seen.

There has been no word of her as yet.

There is a knock at the door. It will be Megumi, ready to leave. She has become more to me than I ever could have imagined.

She is my friend, my girlfriend, my future hope, my sounding board, my compass when I'm lost, my shining light when times are dark.

She is my everything, as I, I hope, am hers.

In two months her year here will be up and she will be leaving for America; we are currently working on ways for her to stay.

When we are in Hiroshima we will go to the site of my home, of Hiro and Keiko's home, her school, and to the memorial service that is to be held.

Will we find Keiko?

I will be taking my book, fewer and fewer pages between the covers. If we do not find her, there will be one fewer page and one more paper crane in this world, sitting next to the memorial mound.

PART THREE

Japan 2018

I stare at my grandfather.
Suddenly he isn't
just my grandfather.

He's a person with a history,
a life.
Who has loved and
was loved in return.
Who was a young man.
A son.
A best friend.

Who was someone's
hope.

'Remember the legend?' he asks.
'You must fold a thousand
paper
cranes
for your wish to come true.

'In the beginning
    my taped-together books held
    nine hundred and
    ninety-nine sheets.

'Now?
    Only the cover remains.'

Questions swim through me.
    I look at him,
    worn down
    by guilt.

'Your grandmother – Megumi –
    was a good person.
    Full of hope.

'But my father,
    your great-grandfather,
    was wrong.
    There is no magic in words.

No magic

in stories.'

'Keiko?'

My voice is a mere wisp of air.

He paces the floor

as I wait.

Through dim light I see

pain,

grief and

guilt

drip from him.

'She is dead,' he says.

Blinds come down over his eyes and

I'm

shut

out.

We form over time.

Products of experience.

Like rocks in the sea.

Silence

    hangs

    like threads.

    Like spider

    webs.

Soles on tatami

    as I follow him from

    kitchen to bedroom,

    his body

    ghosting through

    the air.

'How . . .'

    A word like nails on glass.

    '. . . did you . . .'

    Cracking.

    '. . . find out?'

    Shattering.

His eyes

don't meet mine.

His shoulders

hunch.

His hands

stretch out, holding

a letter between

trembling

fingers.

'I killed her,'

he says.

We lie to ourselves.

We believe it as the truth,

Hold it strong as faith.

Back in the kitchen I am alone.

By the light of the moon

through the window,

I pull the letter from the envelope.

It rustles

and scratches,

the paper old,

and yellowed.

The folds resistant to opening,

threatening to

crumble and

crack,

to destroy its knowledge before

I can be privy.

I ease it with care.

And with fear.

Words jump out.

Enquiry.

Keiko Matsuya.

Hiroshima.

Bomb.

Register.

Survivors.

No record.

Reluctantly conclude

she must have

perished.

I can't look away

from that sentence,

the words

that ate my grandfather's hope.

'Reluctantly conclude she must have

perished.'

Perished.

Perished.

I drop it to the table

and it folds in on

itself once more.

Hiding

its secret

and its

shame.

And I wonder

how many times

he has stared at that sentence.

And I don't want to imagine

the hurt

it caused.

'I'm sorry, Grandfather,'

I whisper.

'I'm sorry.

I'm sorry.

I'm sorry.'

And I wish

with all my soul

that I could fix him.

Challenge memories

So old, so frosted, so blurred.

Look now through clear eyes.

I wake

    to darkness.

    To cold.

    To silence.

My head is on the table

    where I rested it,

    the letter next to me.

    Its words

    echo and

    pound

    through me,

    as they have

    through history.

The clock ticks to five and I stand.

    Through the window,

    under a street light,

    I see a figure.

    Grandfather.

    Staring

into the darkness
of the night sky.

How many people
have told him
it wasn't his fault?
How many would it take
for him to believe it?

One, I think.
But only the right
one.

I glance back to that letter
and I remember specific words.
No record.
Reluctantly conclude.
No
record.

He steps inside,

     his face tinged blue,

     his fingers

     tight,

     his legs

     slow.

'Sit,' I tell him,

     and pass him

     some hot tea.

'What did you do

     after getting this letter?'

     I ask.

     'Where did you go?

     With whom did you speak?'

His fingers fold around his cup.

     His wrinkled mouth

     blows at the steam.

'Nothing,'

    he replies.

    'Nowhere.

    Nobody.

'You read the letter.

    You saw the words.

    You know what it says.

    No record.

    She is dead.

    She is gone.

    The guilt,

    the fault,

    the blame,

    is mine.

    I killed –'

'No!' I shout.

    'No record,

    it says.

No record alive

but . . .

but no record dead.'

He shakes his head.

'She would've . . .'

he says.

'She could've . . .'

he says.

'Somebody . . .

Something . . .

Somewhere . . .'

he stumbles.

He throws his hands in the air.

'All this time,'

he shouts.

'She would've turned up

somewhere!'

'But . . . maybe,'

    I say.

    'Maybe –'

'No!'

    He slams down the cup.

    I hear it crack.

    'False hope

    is worse

    than

    no hope.'

He storms

    from the room

    and I watch

    tea leak across the table and

    drip,

    drip,

    drip

    onto the floor.

Hope built on the sand

Is foolish. Hope built on rock

Is like sun to seeds.

I sleep

    but Grandfather's story haunts me.

    She comes to me,

    Keiko,

    in my dream.

    I stretch out a hand for her to take

    but she slips from me.

    Sadness

    pulls at my bones and

    fills my soul.

I cannot shake it.

    Cannot shake her.

    She is at my side

    when I wake.

    She is in my head

    when I wash.

    She is waiting for me

    while I dress.

Keiko,

 I think,

 He is sorry.

 Let him go.

 Let us go.

While it is his guilt,

 not her ghost,

 that holds him prisoner,

 it is something else

 in me

 that won't let

 go.

And I wonder

 if all those years

 my grandmother felt the same way

 as I do

 now.

And I wonder

    if it is just

    wishful thinking,

    or something

    more.

Questions unanswered
Nag without end. Untiring,
And unshakeable.

I hear my mother

    come in from work.

    And I hear her

    go to bed.

    And with oolong tea at my side

    I flick the switch

    and stare at the screen.

    as the Internet waits for me.

Forums

    and chat rooms.

    Emails

    and messages.

    Phone calls

    and databases.

    And hope.

    Upon

    hope.

    Upon

    foolish

    hope.

'No,'

    they say.

    'Try this,'

    they say.

    'Try here . . .

    Try her . . .

    Try him . . .'

    they say.

    'Have you asked . . . ?

    Have you seen . . . ?

    Have you read . . . ?'

    they ask.

    'Have you thought . . . ?

    Have you wondered . . . ?

    'About this . . .'

    they try.

    'We pray for you.

    We hope for you.

    We cross our fingers for you,'

    they promise.

'You should

    accept

    the

    truth,'

    they advise.

    Finally.

The truth?

    What is that?

The sun rises,

    reaches high.

    Is bright,

    unlike my heart.

My heart tips,

    and heads back down.

    The world darkens.

    And with it,

    my spirits.

'I told you,'

Grandfather says.

'What did you think you could do?'

Mother adds.

'Accept it,' he says.

'Like you have?' I ask.

It is not an end

Until you have shone the lamp

In every corner.

I eat.

I undress.

I lie down,

but I don't sleep.

Something scratches

at my brain.

Knocks at my thoughts.

Keeps me awake.

Tap, tap, tap.

Drip, drip, drip.

Darkness in dream.

Keiko

by the tram.

Wait for me.

I promise

I'll return.

Keiko.

What did you do?

Where did you go?

What happened to you?

Tap, tap, tap.

Drip, drip, drip.

I wake.

Toss and turn.

My brain nags.

Through the walls I hear Grandfather's snores.

How lucky we are

to have him.

That he survived.

How tenuous life is.

How fragile.

And yet, how strong is the

human

spirit.

I wander the house.

I like the night.

The quiet.

The calm.

The uninterrupted sense of freedom

and isolation.

I turn on the computer,

    revisit the same sites.

    How lucky we are,

    I think again,

    that he survived.

What is tapping at my brain?

    What is dripping through my thoughts?

    My fingers

    type in his name on the screen.

    'Ichiro Ando'.

    Hit enter.

    'Survivor', it reads,

    and next to it

    an old photo.

    I smile.

    Reach out to his image.

    And I touch his name.

    Ando.

Touch it.

    The touch

    screen changes.

    A link I hadn't

    seen.

    Or thought about.

And there are

    all

    the people

    with the family name Ando who

    survived Hiroshima.

There is Yoshiko

    and Hiroshi.

    Hiroko and Emiko.

There is

    Masakatsu,

    Kamiko,

Fujio

and Inosuki.

There is

Takato,

Yasujiro,

Yoshi,

and Fujio.

And there is

Keiko.

There is

Keiko Ando.

A pinprick of light

Is all that you need to guide

You from the darkness.

There is

Keiko

Ando.

Dare to lift the stone

To try, to look, to wonder

And to ask, 'What if?'

'Could it be?'

    I think.

    Could it?

    Could it?

Or a ghost?

    A shadow of the past?

    A false hope?

'Keiko Ando',

    I type.

    Too many results.

    'Hiroshima', I add.

The screen refreshes

    and I stare at

    eyes

    staring

    into

    mine.

Curiosity
Grows, spreads, and blossoms into
An epiphany.

The sky is dark

    as my mother walks in.

    By the time I stop talking

    a trace of orange

    peers over the horizon.

'Are you sure?'

    she says to me.

    I shake my head.

'Then we do nothing,' she says.

    'We leave it.

    We let it go.

    We pretend you never saw.'

'But –' I start.

    'But no,' she says.

    'He is old,

    he is weak.

What good would it do now

to raise his hopes

for a maybe?'

'But –'

'But no.'

The sky is bluer as she leaves for work.

But I sit

with my thoughts whirling.

And when the sun is bright,

and when Grandfather's snores have stopped

and he stands in that doorway,

I smile at him.

Rise from the depths of

Darkness to a horizon

Edged yellow, orange.

'Why are you so happy?' he says.

I place his breakfast on the table.

A cup of tea.

A muffin.

His eyes lift.

And from under heavy lids, they squint.

'Why are you looking at me like that?' he asks.

'Grandfather Ichiro,' I say,

'can you still drive?'

A piece of paper

is folded in my hand,

the ink of the address

burning into my palm.

He shrugs.

'You were a good driver,' I tell him.

'A long time ago,' he replies.

'But you liked it,' I say.

His chin lifts

    a fraction

    and his back straightens

    a trace.

'Let's go for a drive,' I say.

    'Let's have an adventure,

    you and I.'

'Why?' he asks.

    'Because,' I say.

    'Because . . .

    Because . . .

    soon

    I will go to university.

    And I want,

    so desperately,

    I want

    memories of you,

    of me,

    of things we have done together.'

He stares and I wait

    for him to say no.

    To realise I'm lying.

    But I can't tell him the

    truth.

    It will break his heart if I am wrong.

    'Far?' he asks.

I hide my smile.

    'An hour,' I say.

    'Or two

    or so.'

    Whatever is going on

    behind his eyes,

    in his head,

    I do not know.

He is silent.

    Lifts his spoon,

    tinks his cup,

    tap, tap, tap.

And from it drips the tea.

Drip, drip, drip.

He glances sideways

at me.

And I see a light in his eyes

that I've not seen for

years.

'Make some food to take,' he says.

The space between words

Where meaning, understanding,

Are loud in our heads.

The car lurches

    into the road.

    Grandfather's feet,

    that danced

    with Grandmother,

    ran on the beach

    with me,

    walked my mother

    to her first job,

    but lost their enthusiasm to grief,

    and to guilt,

    are clumsy on the pedals

    that he has not touched

    for so long.

Grandfather looks

    petrified and

    exhilarated.

He looks

    alive.

'Which way?'

he shouts.

I point and he swings the car

around.

Lightness

in his eyes.

A smile

on his face.

'An adventure?'

he asks.

'Me and you?'

I nod.

'Lead the way!'

And I do.

We are

conspirators!

We are

adventurers!

We wind down

    the windows.

    We whoop

    and we shout.

    We laugh

    and we smile.

    And the road leads us

    on and

    on.

We share the flask.

    We eat the fruit.

    We divide the biscuits

    and the crisps,

    the rice

    and the noodles.

    We devour

    the cake.

    We cover Mother's car

    in crumbs and

    empty packets.

We fill the air

    with songs

    and laughter.

    And still we drive.

Until . . .

    'Your mother will be needing the car.'

    'I am getting tired.'

    'It's time to go home.'

I look at the map.

    'Please,'

    I say.

    'Just a little further.'

    He pulls to the side and

    turns off the radio.

His parchment hands hold mine.

    His hooded eyes stare into my own.

    The lines on his face,

    like the roads on a map,

deepen as I watch him.

'Mizuki,' he says,

'where are we going?

What are we doing?'

In my pocket

    the paper . . .

    with the address . . .

    . . . burns.

    My fingers touch it.

I stare into his eyes,

    and I imagine his life –

    his memories

    of pain

    of loss

    and of guilt –

    that I want so desperately

    to erase.

    But what if I'm wrong?

'It's getting late,'

    he says.

    The roar of the engine,

    his clumsy foot.

'Thank you,' he says,

    'for a good day.

    But now, we go home.'

When is the point at
Which hope turns to foolishness?
And how do we know?

The black road leads

us away.

Promising us

home.

Stealing our

hope.

The clouds

around us

darken.

'Grandfather Ichiro,' I whisper.

'If . . .

If there was a chance . . .

to fix something,

for someone,

to make them happy again,

but it was only a chance,

and it might not work,

what would you do?'

He frowns but says nothing.

'Is it better,' I continue,

'to try for them, but fail,

than to never try at all?

Even if the failure

could cause them

pain?'

The lights turn red.

He stops the car.

Looks at me.

'The purpose would be

to make them happier?' he asks.

'To fix something?

Re-create balance?'

I nod.

'Do you risk it?' I ask.

The silence is solid.

    I cannot breathe in

    or out.

'Your grandmother told me,' he says,

    'that possibility

    should never be ignored.

    To ignore possibility

    is to deny

    hope.

    Without hope,

    we are nothing but husks.'

The lights change.

    Green on his face.

    'To deny someone hope, she told me,

    is to deny them the air they breathe.'

Behind us

a horn blares.

His back straightens.

'You know the way?'

he asks.

A lone cloud obscures

The sun, but a lone cloud does

Pass quickly over.

The road leads us

    out of a town and

    into the countryside.

    The map is heavy in my hands.

He doesn't ask

    how I know

    or what I know.

Fields go by.

    Roads lead off

    left and right.

    Houses appear,

    and disappear.

On

    and on.

    Until, finally,

    a sign announces

    'Hiroshima Prefecture'.

His body stiffens

    and his face tightens.

'Are we close?'

    he asks.

    I nod.

    He follows my directions.

    Hands trembling,

    fingers tightening on the

    steering wheel.

We turn.

    The road narrows.

    'Number sixty-four,' I say.

    Trees appear.

    'Grandfather Ichiro, if I'm wrong . . .'

    He lifts a hand and

    I stop.

He's silent.

    A bungalow at the end of a private track.

Wooden railings and a veranda.

A field in front.

An open garage with wooden doors.

Evening light

    paints

    the field and

    the house,

    the garage and

    the railings,

    with a sepia tinge.

Grandfather pulls to the right and turns off the engine.

We stare at the house for a

    long

    time.

A mist hangs

    on the ground,

    moving slowly,

    like ghosts

searching

for

the

lost.

I wind down the window and

birdsong

filters

in.

I breathe the calm,

the peace,

the trepidation

and the

hope.

'Shall we knock?' I ask.

Grandfather turns to me.

'At this moment, Mizuki,

I am in

heaven.

At this moment,

I can believe that

inside

that

house

is the girl whose safety I was tasked with.

'I can imagine

I did not let down

my friend

nor betray

his trust.

'I can imagine

she is alive and

she is safe.

That she has lived a

long life and

she is

happy.

'While we sit here, I am

 not guilty.

 It is a wondrous moment.'

The last of the day's sun

 stretches down.

 Touches us

 and we are bathed

 in orange.

 We are bathed

 in warmth.

In peace

 we breathe in

 a hope-filled limbo.

 I wish,

 oh how

 I wish,

 it could last

 forever.

But Grandfather has seen something.

    I hear his intake of

    breath,

    see the focus of his

    eyes.

'Look,'

    he gasps.

He steps from the

    car.

Stands

    motionless.

And

    time

    stalls.

I follow his eyeline.

    Strain my gaze through the windscreen.

'Mizuki,' he breathes,

like

wind.

He raises a hand.

Points

to the window.

I focus on

it

and

gasp.

A

paper

crane.

Echoes of actions

Ripple across time, waiting,

Waiting, waiting, till . . .

I stand with him

and he looks at me

with eyes

filled with

fear.

I reach out and

hold his

hand.

My grandfather,

whom I

love

with

all

my

heart.

'Remember,'

I say.

'You didn't let anyone down.

Whether she is there or not,

you were brave,

you were courageous,

you were loyal.'

The storm door to the house swings

open.

A boy – a teenager –

comes out.

On the veranda he stands,

watching us

as we walk towards him.

'Can I help you?'

he asks.

'The crane . . .'

Grandfather begins, shuffling forward.

'The crane . . . on the windowsill?'

The boy

looks from

me

to

Grandfather to

me again.

'We're looking for someone,'

I say.

'Someone

my grandfather knew

a long time ago.

Is this . . . is this . . . the

Ando

residence?'

Slowly,

he nods.

'Yes,'

he says.

His hand is on the door.

'I am Ichiro Ando.'

My stomach lurches.

    Grandfather stumbles and

    grabs my arm.

    We stare at the boy.

    'That,' Grandfather said,

    'is my name.'

Now the boy

    stares

    at

    us.

'My grandmother

    named me,'

    he said,

    'after somebody

    she knew.'

Shivers

    run

    down

    me.

Grandfather stumbles again.
    But the boy is
    there.
    An arm for support and
    a chair to rest,
    and a look on his face of
    sheer
    wonderment.

'The crane . . .'
    My grandfather's voice
    strains and
    breaks.
    He points to the window
    where it sits on the sill.

The edges

are brown.

The characters

are faded.

The handwritten

scrawl down the

margin is

blurred from

years and

years of

waiting.

'It's hers,'

the boy Ichiro says.

'From a long time

ago.'

My eyes

fill with

tears

and my

chest

fills with

hope.

'Are you . . . ?'

the boy Ichiro asks.

'Are you . . .

Ichiro Ando

from Hiroshima?'

My grandfather

looks at the boy

with eyes

filled with guilt.

'Is she here?'

I ask.

And like new shoots desperate

for sunlight,

we stare up at him.

'No,'

he replies.

'But I can take you to her.'

A word, just one word

Of letters and sounds, can change

Lives, and change futures.

The car bumps.

Lurches.

Through suburbs

and into the city.

'She goes every week now,'

Ichiro says.

'Sits all day

on a particular bench.

Staring.

Waiting.

'She's been ill,

on and off,

for years.

They say it's because of

Hiroshima.

'When I was younger,'

he continues,

'and she was too,

she spoke about it –

Hiroshima.

She remembered so much.

She told me about the

boy who

saved

her.

'She said that he rescued her from the

    fire

    and the

    water.

    He told her to rest by a tram while he went for

    help.

'She said that she waited for him.

    But she was

    tired and

    couldn't stay awake.

'She said that she remembered

    closing

    her

    eyes.

    And when she opened

    them

    she was in a

    shelter.

'The first word she said was

    Ando.

    They thought that was her

    family name.

    They wrote it on the sheet

    and she never

    corrected them.

    A mark of respect

    to the boy

    who

    saved

    her.

'She no longer remembers
    her old family name.

'She told me that
    he gave her the crane
    when he went for
    help.
    It has sat on her windowsill
    for as long as I can
    remember.

'A symbol of thanks
    and remembrance.
    Or perhaps
    of hope.'

In the mirror he looks at
    Grandfather.
    'Thank you,'
    he says.

Grandfather is

    silent,

    watching through the window

    as houses

    and buildings,

    trees

    and flowers,

    and

    life

    pass us by.

But I see those words

    sink into

    his

    skin.

    And I see them

    water

    a heart

    that since Grandmother died

    has been

    barren.

Ichiro pulls in near the

    train station

    and shadows of

    history

    sweep over

    Grandfather's face.

'It will be easier

    to walk from here,'

    Ichiro says.

    'I will guide you.'

'No,'

    Grandfather says to Ichiro.

    'Wait here.

    I know where she will be

    and I know the way

    like the back of my

    hand.'

Look straight ahead with
A nod to the past and an
Eye on the future.

'The park was there,'

    he says as we walk.

    'And that was the river we stood in.'

    He points.

    'This is the road we walked down

    that didn't

    look much like a

    road

    back then.

    The school there,'

    he says,

    'was the first school your

    grandmother and I

    visited

    when we came looking for her.

'We walked this

    exact

    way

    together.

Just as I did with

Keiko.'

He pulls an

old

battered

book

from his pocket.

Only the

front cover

and

back cover

remain.

'The Tale of Genji,'

I say as we walk.

'The book your

father

gave you

when he went to

war.

The pages you

turned into

paper

cranes.'

'One more crane

to make,'

he replies.

'Over there,'

he says,

'is the memorial.

For thirty years I went,

until

I couldn't face it

any more.

I'd hoped to see her,

but

never did.'

'Perhaps she never went?'
    I say.
    'Perhaps she couldn't face
    you
    not being there.'

We cross the road.
    We're following the
    tram tracks.
    We turn a corner.

Some distance ahead,
    to the side of the tracks,
    is a
    bench.

Grandfather's feet
    stop.

Pain, for many, is

Accepted, necessary

Punishment for guilt.

'Is that where you left her?' I ask.

He nods.

'Let's go closer,' I say,

but his feet

are rigid.

'I can't.'

His voice quivers.

'I can't,'

he repeats.

'All this time,

these years.

'What if . . .

she isn't here?

What if . . .

she hates me?

What if . . . ?'

Crowds swirl around us,

oblivious to this

old man

and his

decades of

pain.

I see his eyes

leap to

the past.

He is seventeen again.

Full of uncertainty

and fear.

And a decision he must make.

'I can't,' he says.

'I don't . . .

know . . .

how.'

Yet I know

from the story he told

and the life he has lived

that he is

full

of

courage.

'Yes, you do,'
    I whisper.
    And I take his book,
    rip off the front cover and
    pass it to him.

'Do the same as you did
    back then,' I say.

He nods,
    and he blinks back his tears,
    and while his fingers
    force the old paperback cover
    into clumsy creases and
    folds,
    we move through the crowd,

ever closer to

that

bench.

And suddenly

I

catch

my

breath.

A woman

sits

there.

Small,

grey hair pulled back,

one hand holding something,

the other

drumming a

rhythm on her leg.

Tap,

    tap,

    tap.

Drip,

    drip,

    drip.

A shiver runs

    through me and

    I feel

    Grandfather stand just a

    little

    taller.

She

    rests her hands on her

    lap and

    her

    fingers

move slowly,
intricately.

Then she stops.
And she looks at
something
in her outstretched
palm.

'What is that?'
I ask.
'What has she made?'

Grandfather
is
speechless.

'Grandfather Ichiro?'
I say.

'It's . . . a . . .'

    he whispers.

    'It's . . . a

    paper

    crane.'

Suddenly she

    looks up at

    Grandfather,

    and at the

    paper crane

    he holds

    between his fingers.

The world around us

    pauses.

A thousand paper
Cranes, for hope, truth, dignity,
For wishes, for peace.

I watch my grandfather,

    his parchment fingers

    holding the

    bird's

    wing

    as he walks

    towards

    her.

She's watching

    every

    single

    step

    he

    takes,

    and his eyes

    have not

    left

    her.

He stops at the bench,

    sits next to her.

    And the look

    between them

    is something there are

    no words

    for on this

    earth.

For an

    eternity

    they don't move

    or take their

    eyes

    from

    each

    other.

He lifts her hand,

    and in it

    places the

crane

he's just made,

and her

fingers

brush it with

such

care.

He touches her face

and they smile.

After so many

years,

and so much

waiting,

they are finally

together.

Dare to promise and
Dare to wish, dare to dream and
Dare to hope, always.

I want to be privy to their

conversation.

I want to hear her refuse his

apologies.

Hear the unburdening of his

guilt

and the acceptance of his own

release.

I want to hear her

story.

What has happened to her

since.

What her

life

has been.

But that

place

on that

bench,

right now,

    is not for

    me.

It is

    their time.

I take one last glance at the crane in her hand –

    the

    last

    paper

    crane –

    before I turn

    and walk away.

Their circle

    is complete.

But their story

will

ripple

through

time

forever.

ACKNOWLEDGEMENTS

I'd especially like to thank Kahori Wada at the Hiroshima Peace Memorial Museum, who answered many of my questions and provided me with links to exhibits, brochures, maps and other documents; Gaye Rowley, researcher of Japanese literature and the history of women in Japan, lecturer in Japanese Literature at Wasada University and Associate Director of their library; Zack Davisson, Japanese–English translator, writer, and scholar of Japanese folklore. And of course, the Atomic Bomb Museum.

Any factual errors are mine alone.

For anyone who would like to read more about Hiroshima, I'd recommend beginning with these and seeing where they lead you –

Hiroshima by John Hersey

Black Rain by Masuji Ibuse

Hiroshima Diary: The Journal of a Japanese Physician by Michihiko Hachiya

Thanks also to Natsko Seki, whose illustrations have brought this story, and my words, to life more than I could've hoped for.

This little book has a long history, and two people in particular have supported it in all its transformations and stages. Without them my head would be more stressed, and my ambition would be muted. Thank you, Rebecca Mascull and Emma Pass – your support and friendship have helped *Paper Crane* become what it is.

Taking the manuscript down from the shelf it had sat on for three years and handing it over to Emma Matthewson was a frightening prospect. Emma, your enthusiasm and belief in it brought me to tears – giving life to a project I'd thought would never see the light of day. I couldn't have asked for a more insightful, considered, patient and understanding editor – thank you.

Working on an illustrated book with parts written in free verse has presented challenges I've never come across before, and so I'd like to thank both

Talya Baker and Sophie McDonnell for their unwavering patience, support and understanding. This book is better for their input.

Thanks also to my wonderful agent, Jane Willis, for reading drafts of this, being a sounding board, and always in my corner.

Of course thanks too go to everyone both at Hot Key and at United Agents.

I've been very fortunate to have had the support of some wonderful independent bookshops, and thanks go to Drakes in Stockton-on-Tees, the Book Fayre in Woodhall Spa and Lindum Books in Lincoln. Thanks also to school librarians Eileen Armstrong, Lorraine Gill, Kath Jago and Jess McFarlane.

Thanks to those who took the time to speak to me about their own memories of the Cold War – so many, but especially Matt Naylor and Jim Parker.

To fellow authors, thank you for the support and the laughs: Chris Callaghan, Jo Nadin, Zoe Marriott, Sheena Wilkinson, Eve Ainsworth, Liz Kessler, Gordon Smith, Helen Grant, Paula Rawsthorne, Rachel Ward, Sally Nicholls, Caroline

Green, Rhian Ivory, Susie Day, Keris Stainton, Fiona Dunbar, Katy Moran, Shirley McMillan, Dan Smith, James Nicol, Leila Rasheed, Keren David and Rae Earl.

To the Savvy Authors for the group support and encouragement.

To fellow Prime Writers, including Louise Beech, Louisa Treger, Sarah Jasmon, Emma Curtis, Karin Salvalaggio, Katherine Clements, Keith Mansfield, Essie Fox, Jon Teckman, Antonia Honeywell, Sarah Taylor and Rachael Lucas.

To my Happy Place comrades – Beth Miller, Kerry Hadley, Melissa Bailey, Rebecca Mascull – for the laughs, the canaries and the coal mines.

Outside of writing, thanks to my fellow Double Brutal finisher Martin Ball, whose distraction is welcome and inspiration appreciated. You've pushed me to achieve what I never thought could be possible. Here's to returning to Mordor sometime – it'll be a challenging journey, but I know the company will be good.

Thanks also to my 2019 Iron chums – Tracey Wilkinson, Daniela Dumitrescu and Rob Keep. And to Carl Wilkinson who is always interested and curious.

Finally to family – Helen and Patrick Megginson, Janet and Jack Baron, Colin, Dad and Ann, Meghan.

And of course to Jess, Danny, Bowen and Russ – you are my world.

A Note from the Illustrator

What motivated me throughout this project was a sense of responsibility as a Japanese illustrator. I grew up in Japan, and the story of Hiroshima had been told many times. I strongly remember the horrendous visual and emotional impact I felt as a child whenever I heard or read about the bomb.

For this book, I spent many hours on visual research, conscious that my illustrations could become the first visual encounter with the harrowing event for some readers. Although my illustrations are about the day of the bomb and the days after, the other thing I focused on was to deliver the atmosphere of Ichiro's emotional journey, which starts on the day and carries on throughout the book, as this story is unlike any other ones I've read, a unique piece of work about human relationships set in contemporary Japan as well as around the time of the bomb.

I enjoyed creating circular brush strokes for the haiku. They were drawn using Japanese calligraphy brush and ink, which my son has been using at Japanese language school in London. I used to learn calligraphy when I was a child, and it was so emotional for me to realise I could still remember how to move my arm in just the right way to make the very specific brushstrokes required.

Natsko Seki

Kerry Drewery is the author of the CELL 7 trilogy, the first of which won the Spellbinding Book of the Year 2018 and has been translated into more than a dozen languages, as well as two other highly acclaimed YA novels: *A Brighter Fear* (2012) (which was Love Reading 4 Kids Book of the Month and shortlisted for the Leeds Book Award) and *A Dream of Lights* (2013) (nominated for the CILIP Carnegie Medal, awarded Highly Commended at the North East Teen Book Awards and shortlisted for the Hampshire Independent Schools Book Awards). Both were published by HarperCollins in the UK and Callenbach in the Netherlands.

NATSKO SEKI is a Japanese illustrator whose work has been featured in many magazines, including the *Financial Times* magazine. Her published books include *Architecture According to Pigeons* and *On a Double Decker Bus*.

How to Fold a Traditional Crane

The traditional Japanese art of paper-folding to create different shapes is called origami. There are thousands of different shapes, traditional and modern. Any square piece of paper is suitable to use, but thin paper is best, and many people like to use coloured or patterned paper.

You can find a sheet of origami paper at the back of this book. Tear it out carefully and make each fold as precisely as you can. You will probably need to make several paper cranes before yours looks really good, so you might want to practise on plain paper.

If you find it easier to follow instructions from a video, there are many on the Internet, including instructions for making an exact square and for folding many different shapes. For a paper crane, go to **tinyurl.com/nanfmko**

KEY

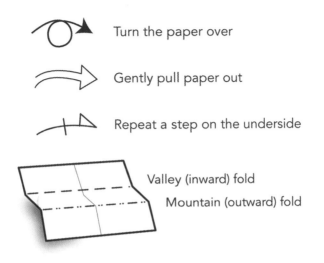

Turn the paper over

Gently pull paper out

Repeat a step on the underside

Valley (inward) fold

Mountain (outward) fold

INSTRUCTIONS

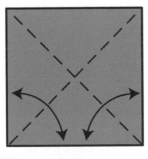

① Coloured side up, crease and unfold both diagonals.

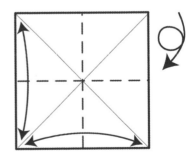

② Turn the paper over, crease in half and unfold both ways.

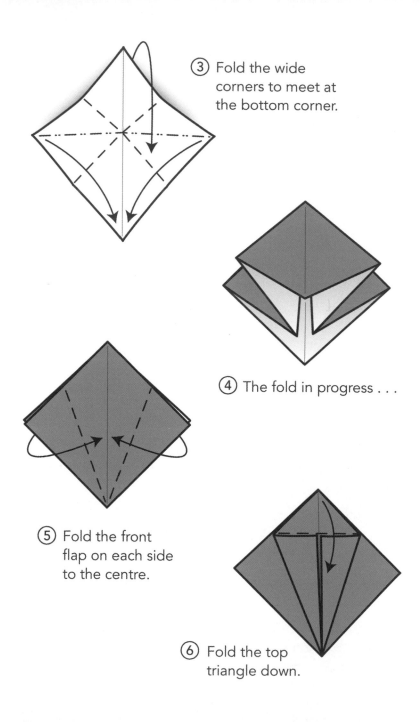

3 Fold the wide corners to meet at the bottom corner.

4 The fold in progress . . .

5 Fold the front flap on each side to the centre.

6 Fold the top triangle down.

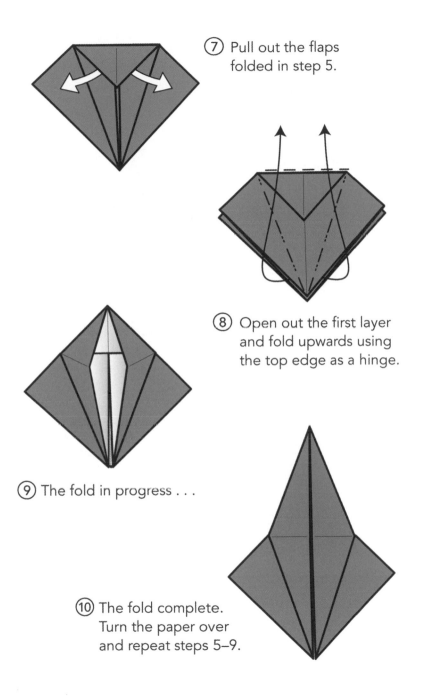

⑦ Pull out the flaps folded in step 5.

⑧ Open out the first layer and fold upwards using the top edge as a hinge.

⑨ The fold in progress . . .

⑩ The fold complete. Turn the paper over and repeat steps 5–9.

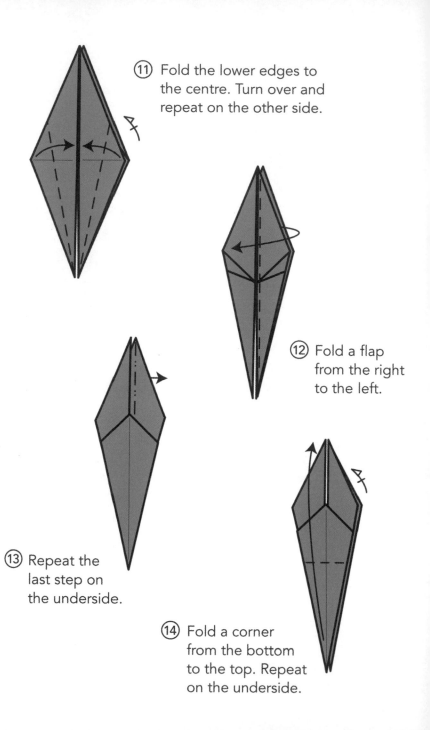

⑪ Fold the lower edges to the centre. Turn over and repeat on the other side.

⑫ Fold a flap from the right to the left.

⑬ Repeat the last step on the underside.

⑭ Fold a corner from the bottom to the top. Repeat on the underside.

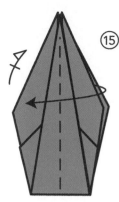

(15) Fold the upper right flap to the left. Repeat on the underside.

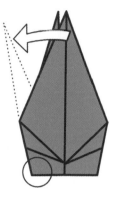

(16) Hold the circled area with one hand and pull the central flap to the left with the other hand. Flatten into position.

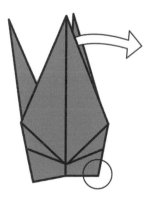

(17) Repeat the last step on the right.

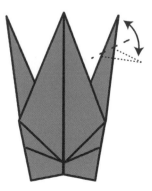

(18) Fold and unfold the beak.

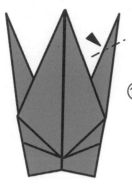

19 Push the beak inwards and downwards, then pinch when in position.

20 Carefully ease the wings out and down, gently pressing the centre point to partially flatten it.

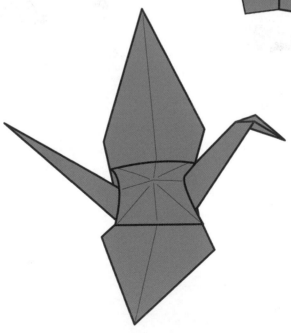